It was a Norman Rockwell picture, all warm and fuzzy.

She saw father and daughter sitting just inside the barn, busily cleaning Lanie's bridle and saddle.

Though Shaunna had sworn off men, she would admit there were times when she thought of being married, having children and watching them with their father. This was one of those times.

Not that Tyler would fit in that picture, she knew. She and Tyler were as opposite as they came.

Which was why she couldn't understand why she found him so attractive. All night she'd thought about his kiss. Lying in her bed, she'd tossed and turned, playing it over and over in her head and wondering how far they would have gone if she hadn't stopped him.

Wondering if she should have stopped him...

Dear Reader,

Silhouette Romance novels aren't just for other women—the wonder of a Silhouette Romance is that it can touch *your* heart. And this month's selections are guaranteed to leave you smiling!

In Suzanne McMinn's engaging BUNDLES OF JOY title, *The Billionaire and the Bassinet,* a blue blood finds his hardened heart irrevocably tamed. This month's FABULOUS FATHERS offering by Jodi O'Donnell features an emotional, heartwarming twist you won't soon forget; in *Dr. Dad to the Rescue,* a man discovers strength and the healing power of love from one *very* special lady. *Marrying O'Malley,* the renegade who'd been her childhood nemesis, seemed the perfect way for a bride-to-be to thwart an unwanted betrothal—until their unlikely alliance stirred an even more incredible passion; don't miss this latest winner by Elizabeth August!

The Cowboy Proposes...Marriage? Get the charming lowdown as WRANGLERS & LACE continues with this sizzling story by Cathy Forsythe. Cara Colter will make you laugh and cry with *A Bride Worth Waiting For,* the story of the boy next door who *didn't* get the girl, but who'll stop at nothing to have her now. For readers who love powerful, dramatic stories, you won't want to miss *Paternity Lessons,* Maris Soule's uplifting FAMILY MATTERS tale.

Enjoy this month's titles—and please drop me a line about *why* you keep coming back to Romance. I want to make sure we continue fulfilling *your* dreams!

Regards,

Mary-Theresa Hussey

Mary-Theresa Hussey
Senior Editor Silhouette Romance

Please address questions and book requests to:
Silhouette Reader Service
U.S.: 3010 Walden Ave., P.O. Box 1325, Buffalo, NY 14269
Canadian: P.O. Box 609, Fort Erie, Ont. L2A 5X3

PATERNITY LESSONS

Maris Soule

Silhouette
ROMANCE™
Published by Silhouette Books
America's Publisher of Contemporary Romance

My thanks to my cousin, Donal Mettler, for his assistance.
I'd forgotten what it was like to have horses in California.
And my respect to all of those horse trainers who have
learned to "listen" to horses, especially to Monty Roberts,
Ray Hunt, Pat Parelli and John Lyons, who have spread
the word through clinics and their writings.

 SILHOUETTE BOOKS

ISBN 0-373-19389-0

PATERNITY LESSONS

This edition published by arrangement with Harlequin Books S.A.

® and TM are trademarks of Harlequin Books S.A., used under license.
Trademarks indicated with ® are registered in the United States Patent
and Trademark Office, the Canadian Trade Marks Office and in other
countries.

Visit us at www.romance.net

Printed in U.S.A.

MARIS SOULE

was born in California, but now lives in Michigan with her husband and family. The author of numerous category romances, she is now happy to be writing for the Silhouette Romance line. Maris believes that marriage takes a lot of commitment and energy, but it is the best thing that can happen to a person. When Maris and her husband married, they decided to take one year at a time, renewing their "unwritten" contract each May. So far they've renewed it twenty-four times—not bad in this day and age!

Dear Reader,

I've always loved horses, and my daughter, Mia, inherited that love. We bought Mia her first horse when she was eleven, a half-Arab who's taught us a lot and still lives with us. We read the horse magazines, made mistakes, slowly learned and our "stable" increased to three horses. My husband and I were the grooms and financial supporters, our daughter the rider and trainer. It was a family affair.

Writing this book allowed me to remember those times—my panic when Mia was thrown off and got a concussion, and my pride when she and a half-Arab she'd trained placed Top Ten in the Arab Nationals. In *Paternity Lessons,* a traumatized Mustang brings a father and his daughter together with a horse trainer—a horse whisperer—and in the process, all three learn the meaning of family.

Enjoy!

Maris Soule

Chapter One

Tyler Corwin knew that Robin Leach wouldn't be showing this house on *Lifestyles of the Rich and Famous*. The edges of the concrete steps were crumbling, the wooden porch had creaked when he stepped on it, and the screen door hung at an angle, an inch-wide gap at the top allowing easy access to the flies circling around his head. Through the screening, he watched a middle-aged Hispanic woman, almost as broad as she was tall, waddle toward him. She stopped on the other side of the screen door but made no effort to open it.

"I'm looking for a Shaunna Lightfeather," he said. "I'm Tyler Corwin. I called earlier. She's expecting me."

He got a grunt and the woman turned away, speaking as she waddled back into the kitchen. "She's changing. She said for you to wait in the kitchen."

Assuming he was on his own to enter, Tyler pulled open the screen door. Its hinges creaked, and the moment he stepped inside, he caught the smell of horse manure and heard the strains of a country-and-western song. Scattered around on the floor to his left were several pairs of cowboy boots, all scuffed and showing years of wear. To his right, on a washing machine, were a pair of soiled jeans and a stained plaid cotton shirt.

He wrinkled his nose at the smell, then gave a chuckle as the screen door banged closed behind him. This was certainly different from the clean hallways and offices of the accounting firm of Smith and Fischer. The ten-mile drive from downtown Bakersfield had put him into another world, a world that up until six months ago he hadn't been aware even existed.

As he made his way into the kitchen, the Hispanic woman motioned toward a Formica-topped table half-covered with papers and horse magazines. Taking that as an invitation to sit there, he pulled out a chair. The plastic on the seat was taped over in two places, its golden color faded and discolored. "Coffee?" the woman asked.

Tyler could smell the brew as well as see the half-filled pot. He suspected it had been strong to begin with and had been sitting there for hours. He smiled politely and shook his head. "No thanks."

Again the woman grunted. "She'll be out soon."

Saying no more, she left the room, her brightly patterned cotton skirt swinging with the sway of her ample hips. Tyler watched her disappear, then glanced around.

The wood-framed house was a sprawling ranch style that mimicked many built after World War II and was definitely showing its age. The wallpaper was dingy, the linoleum worn and cracked, the sink faucet dripping. From everything he'd seen so far, it didn't look as if money was in abundance at this stable. He considered that to be in his favor. If the owner needed money, he should be able to convince her to take on another horse...even one like Magic.

"Mr. Corwin?"

The throaty sound of his name pulled his attention toward the back of the house. His gaze locked onto a woman in her late twenties, and he took in a breath.

Tall and slender, she stood in the doorway with her legs slightly apart, her hands on her hips and her chin high. Her blue jeans were snug but not tight, and the cream-colored corduroy shirt she was wearing was cut like a man's, the sleeves rolled up to her elbows. The top buttons were open, leaving a V that drew his gaze to her chest, and though he wouldn't call her busty, he could see a definite cleavage. He found himself wondering if she was wearing a bra, the thought surprising him. He also felt an increase in his pulse, which was another surprise. He wasn't a man easily excited by a woman.

He attributed his response to her striking looks. Her skin was a rich golden-brown that reflected both hours spent in the sun and a Native American heritage. And perhaps to show that heritage, in the mane of thick brown hair that cascaded down past her shoulders was one slender braid intertwined with yarn and finished with two feathers. More than anything, it was her eyes that caught his attention. Though he supposed they could be classified as brown, the color topaz better described them in his mind.

He stood to greet her. "Ms. Lightfeather?"

In rising, he knocked over his chair, the metal frame clattering against the linoleum, the sound jarring his composure. She merely smiled and stepped into the kitchen. "Call me Shaunna. Sorry to keep you waiting. A colt I'm working with pushed me into a pile of manure, and I decided it was in our best interest if I changed."

He would call her anything she wanted—he needed her help—but he hadn't expected her to be this young...or this beautiful. Quickly, he righted his chair. "Obviously, I'm

Tyler Corwin, the one who called. Just call me Tyler. And I appreciate your taking time to see me.''

"You didn't give me much of a choice." She smiled and stopped a few feet away, close enough that he caught the clean scent of soap. She'd done more than simply changed clothes.

When she held out her right hand, he shook it. Her grip was firm, and that didn't surprise him. She had the look of a woman who would be assertive and strong. But he did note how different her hand felt from the smooth palms of the women he did business with. Holding Shaunna Lightfeather's hand was nothing like holding Alicia Fischer's, the woman he'd been dating for almost a year.

The calluses on Shaunna's palm, he was sure, were from hard manual labor, something he doubted Alicia would ever know. Alicia had been born with a silver spoon in her mouth, and even now, in her position as an event coordinator, a telephone was about the heaviest item she picked up. Her strength was in her mind, she always said.

What did surprise Tyler was the urge that swept through him to hold on to Shaunna's hand, to capture a bit of the strength he sensed in her. Quickly, he released his hold and rubbed his palms together.

"Sit down." Shaunna gestured toward the chair he'd righted. "Coffee?" Again he refused, and she smiled. "Probably a wise decision. Maria makes a strong cup of coffee to begin with. By afternoon, it's deadly." She sat across from him. "So tell me about this horse you mentioned on the phone. It's your daughter's horse?"

"Yes. Actually, technically, I guess, it still belongs to the Bureau of Land Management. It's a wild Mustang."

"On the phone you said you'd had the horse a year. Shouldn't you be getting title to him soon?"

"I...I guess so."

She smiled at his hesitancy. "Have you contacted them? Asked for title to him?"

"I...that is..."

Shaunna watched Tyler Corwin shift position in his chair. When he called earlier, he'd said he would be coming from his office, so she wasn't surprised that he was wearing a suit. The cut was good on him, the dark blue pinstripe accentuating a nice set of shoulders. His white shirt and red-and-blue tie were conservative. He'd explained that he was an accountant, a CPA. She wondered if he was honest. She needed someone to do her books, but she wasn't going to make the same mistake she'd made before.

Again, he shifted his position. "There's a small problem," he finally said.

Anytime someone said there was a "small problem," she knew it wasn't going to be small. "What kind of problem?"

"The horse is...that is..." He hesitated. "Perhaps I should explain a few things."

He looked directly into her eyes, and she could practically see her reflection in those pools of blue. Though she'd classify him as overall good-looking, his eyes, she decided, were his best feature. And maybe his hair. It was a sandy-blond, thick and obviously cut by a barber who knew how to tame it into a proper business style. That kind of hair tempted a touch. Invited a little messing up.

Not that she was tempted.

"Explain away," she said, determined to keep her mind on the horse and not his hair.

"Well, as I said on the phone, Lanie was in an accident six months ago, and—"

"Lanie's your daughter?" She thought that was the name he'd said in their earlier conversation.

Her interruption seemed to catch him off guard, and he

hesitated before going on. "Ah...yes. She was in a car accident with her mother and stepfather. It was a drunk driver. The guy drove head-on into the car. Lanie's mother—my ex-wife—and Lanie's stepfather were killed instantly. Lanie was in the back seat. For a while, we didn't think she'd live. She had to stay in the hospital for a month. Since then, she's been recuperating both physically and mentally."

Shaunna nodded. Losing a mother and stepfather would be a traumatic event for a child. "You said you've boarded the horse during this time."

"Yes." He shook his head. "It was the only thing I could do. I know nothing about horses, except what I've been learning recently. I didn't even know Lanie had a horse, not until my ex's next-door neighbors came to the hospital and told me. No one was feeding or watering the horse and they were concerned about his welfare. They were the ones who suggested I board him somewhere until I decided what to do with him. So that's what I did."

"Sounds reasonable. And the place you chose is where he's at now?"

"Yes." He grimaced. "It's a stable on the other side of Bakersfield. He's been there for five and a half months now. I thought he'd be fine, be taken care of, so I didn't really do anything about him except pay his board bill when it arrived each month. I just didn't have time to check on him, not between the time I was spending with Lanie and my job."

"But now you have seen him." At least, that was what he'd said on the phone.

"Yes. Last week. Lanie and I went to visit the stable. Her doctor felt it would be a good idea if she spent some time with her horse, that it would help her deal with all that happened. But it wasn't a good idea. Lanie got very upset when she saw him, and I was shocked. The horse is in terrible shape.''

"By terrible shape you mean—''

"Dirty. Filthy dirty.'' Tyler's tone held disgust, and he shook his head. "They said he kept breaking out of his paddock, so they put him in a stall. A stall built like a tomb. I don't think he's been out of it in months, or that they've cleaned it in months. It was a mess. And the smell...'' He wrinkled his nose. "I couldn't believe the condition that horse was in when I saw him.''

If the horse was being kept where she thought it might be, Shaunna could believe what he was saying. He'd picked a name out of a phone book and naively assumed the stable owners would do as they promised. And they should have. Problem was, not all did. "You say they haven't let this horse out of that stall for months?''

"I don't think so. The way it looked and smelled, he's just been locked in there.''

"Can the horse even walk?'' She'd seen some abused horses that couldn't.

"Oh, he can walk,'' Tyler said firmly, then stood and left the table, going toward the window in the kitchen that looked out at her barns and arenas. There he stopped and stared through it, and she heard him give a deep sigh before he turned back to her. "The horse can do more than walk. The moment we opened the door to take him out, he lunged for Lanie. Actually, he tried to attack her.''

"Attack?'' Shaunna shook her head. "I'd say you do have a problem.'' And it wasn't a "small'' one. "How old did you say your daughter is? Ten?''

"Just.''

"A child that young shouldn't have a horse like that. A child needs a quiet horse. Something safe.''

"I know. And I'm all for getting rid of this horse, but

Lanie insists he wasn't this way before the accident...before he was sent to this stable. She says her mother had someone come to their place and break the horse. Before the accident, Lanie was riding him all the time and he was safe and gentle.''

Shaunna grimaced at the word "break." So often, that was what happened. The trainer did break the horse's spirit. Instead of a companion and partner, the rider had a slave.

And sometimes the slave rebelled.

"As I said," Tyler continued, "no matter what the horse was like before, considering how he is now, I think we should get rid of him. Sell him or send him back to where he came from. The problem is, Lanie's doctor feels it's important for her to have this horse right now. The doctor says because Lanie's mother got the horse for her, getting rid of him would adversely affect Lanie's recovery, that she needs the horse both emotionally and physically. So on one hand, for Lanie's sake, we need to keep the horse. But on the other hand, he's too crazy to keep. I'm not sure what to do. I know the horse can't be left where he is, but for anyone to handle him, he has to be tamed.''

Shaunna smiled. "So you called me hoping that I'd take him in and tame him?''

Tyler studied her for a moment, then walked back to his chair. "I must admit you're younger than I expected, but since that day we went to see the horse, I've been asking around, and everyone I've talked to says you're the best horse trainer in the area...in the state of California. That you can work miracles with a horse.''

She started to protest, but he went on. "They say that you have the touch...that what you do is pure magic. Lanie calls this horse Magic. I'd say he needs a little.''

"From what you've told me, I'd say he needs a lot.''

"He's not getting it where he's at," Tyler said, "And

I'm afraid if we leave him there, he's not going to. The day after Lanie and I saw him, I went back to the stable and talked to the owner. She feels the best way to handle the horse is to starve him until he's too weak to fight us. And, from the looks of him, I'd say that's exactly what she's been doing.'' He shook his head. ''But no more. I will not starve or abuse an animal, no matter how vicious he might be. I told her she'd better make sure Magic got his full ration of food from now on and that he'd be out of there within a week.'' Tyler sighed, then smiled ruefully. ''So, will you take him?''

Shaunna was now sure, from what he'd said, that she knew exactly where the horse was being kept. She'd heard dozens of horror stories about that stable. As far as she was concerned, the place should be condemned and the owners put into cells and starved. It would serve them right to be treated the same way as they treated the horses.

And she appreciated Tyler's desire to get his horse out of a bad situation, liked the firmness of his voice and admired his dogged determination to talk her into seeing him this afternoon, even though she'd said she was busy. He might not know anything about horses, but he was obviously a caring person. Not that that lessened her problem. ''As I said on the phone when you called, I don't have any free stalls or paddocks, and I won't for another two months.''

He kept his gaze locked with hers. ''I can't leave him where he is.''

''There are other stables around Bakersfield.''

''And do you think they could handle a horse like this? Could they make him safe for Lanie to handle?''

Without knowing the horse, she wasn't sure how to answer, but from what Tyler had said, she knew few could.

''These past six months haven't been easy for Lanie,''

he said. "First losing her mother and stepfather, then being in a hospital for a month, and finally having to come live with me...a virtual stranger. Lanie..." He paused, then looked down at the linoleum.

Shaunna watched him run his fingers through his hair, mussing the neat cut. Finally, he looked up. "Lanie is very angry right now, and we aren't getting along very well. Her doctor says she's lashing out because she's hurting, and since I'm close, I'm the target. I don't want to have to tell her I had to send the horse back."

"No, it probably wouldn't be a good idea," she agreed. "And if you do send him back, there's a good chance he'll become dog food." Which Shaunna didn't want to see happen to any horse.

And she felt she understood his daughter's anger. With Tyler and his wife divorced, it wouldn't be unusual for the mother to make the ex-husband into the bad guy. Shaunna's mother had certainly bad-mouthed her father often enough, both when he was around and after he'd gone. The children of divorce usually were angry, Shauna knew.

In her case, she'd been angry with both of her parents. With her mother for being the person she was, and with her father for leaving her. Maybe he hadn't died, but he might as well have. Not once did she hear from him after he took off. No birthday cards. No Christmas presents. Nothing.

"I'll pay extra," Tyler said.

Shaunna shook off the memories of her past. "If I help you, and I'm not saying I will, it isn't going to be for the money."

His gaze turned to a stack of unpaid bills on the table. "A little extra might help."

Probably, though she had no idea exactly what her financial situation was. She did know she'd be making a lot more money if she wasn't always rescuing animals others had given up on. Horses. Dogs. Cats. At least if she did take on this horse, it wouldn't be for free.

"I have a feeling you're Magic's only hope," Tyler said, the softening of his tone touching her as no offer of money ever would.

He was getting to her with those intense blue eyes of his and the fact that he cared. She was intrigued by the prospect of working with a wild Mustang gone bad, and she was intrigued by Tyler Corwin. "I'll have to go see the horse," she said. "There are some I can't help."

"All I'm asking is that you try," Tyler said, his smile growing wider. "If you can just get him to the stage where Lanie can handle him."

"You said her doctor feels the horse will help her physically as well as emotionally. How is her physical health?" Shaunna asked. "Is she fit enough to work with this horse?"

"Yes. She has a slight limp and hasn't regained all of her strength, but her doctor feels riding will help strengthen her muscles."

"From what you've told me, she won't be riding the horse for a while. But I'd expect her to work with him on a daily basis, especially in the beginning."

"If that's what it takes, she'll be here. All I ask is that you not put her in any danger. I do care about her."

"I'll want to see the horse and meet her before I make a decision."

"You want to meet her? Lanie?" Shaunna noted a flash of panic in his look and had a feeling there was something he wasn't telling her. At the lift of her eyebrows, he quickly acquiesced. "Okay," he said. "You tell me when, and we'll be here."

"How about Saturday? Say ten o'clock?"

"Saturday, ten o'clock it is."

Tyler left the house with mixed feelings. He was sure once Shaunna saw Lanie's horse, she would move the Mustang to her stable. If what he'd heard about her was true, she wouldn't allow that horse to spend two more minutes, much less two months or even two days, in his current condition. Even he didn't want that, and he was no horse lover.

What worried him was taking Lanie to meet Shaunna. He knew how Lanie acted around Alicia, how she acted around him. Lanie's doctor said Lanie's behavior was her way of testing him.

Well, she certainly was.

The battle was constant, and he sometimes wondered if it was worth it. Lanie was so angry, and nothing he said seemed to help. Nothing he did made a difference.

Yet he couldn't give up. He still remembered how she'd been as a baby, smiling when he went to take her out of her crib and reaching for him with those tiny, chubby hands of hers. She'd loved him then, just as he'd loved her. One way or another, he was going to find a means of breaking through the wall she had erected…that fate had erected.

He wondered if he should have told Shaunna the whole story about Lanie. It might have helped her understand things. Then again, he hadn't told Alicia. He hadn't told anyone but his parents and Lanie's doctor. It seemed better that way.

Somehow he would find a way to get past Lanie's anger. And perhaps her doctor was right. Perhaps the horse would help. Perhaps Shaunna Lightfeather would help.

He smiled when he thought of Shaunna. He'd been attracted to her, which he found surprising. Not that she didn't have an appeal. With her high cheekbones, swarthy coloring and unusual eyes, she was a good-looking woman, in a natural sort of way. Striking. Sexy.

He shook his head as he drove back toward Bakersfield. He was thinking crazy. One thing he'd discovered in his thirty-four years was that physical attraction was not enough. And from what little he'd learned and observed about Shaunna, he knew she wasn't a woman who would fit into his life-style. Not at all.

She definitely wasn't a businesswoman. Stacking bills on a kitchen table wasn't a good business practice, and when she'd shown him around her stable, after agreeing to "look" at Magic, Tyler had found himself both impressed and dismayed. On the positive side, although the stable showed its age, everything was neat, in good repair and clean. There were no smelly, dark, tomblike stalls in either of her two barns, and from the looks of her fencing, he didn't think any horse—wild Mustang or not—would be getting out.

And she'd been right when she told him that every stall she had was filled. It was when she said that half of the horses belonged to her—were basically abandoned horses she'd rescued—that he began to understand why so many of those bills on her kitchen table were marked as overdue and why she'd asked if he knew a good accountant, one who was honest. Emotions rather than good business sense seemed to rule her decisions. Emotions he wasn't above playing on.

Nope, from his initial impressions, he wouldn't say Shaunna Lightfeather was a good businesswoman at all. But it didn't hurt his ego to know that she'd found him attractive. At least, her actions made him think she did. It was the only explanation he could give for what happened when she accidentally backed into him, bumping her rear end into his hips.

She'd gotten all flustered and pulled away as if burned by a hot poker. She'd actually blushed, the color turning her skin a richer tan. He'd found her behavior appealing. It had been a while since he'd seen a woman blush.

Appealing, but inconsequential, he told himself. After all, what did they have in common? She loved animals, had them all over the place: dogs, cats, horses and cattle. There was even a baby bird that had fallen out of its nest. He hadn't owned a pet since the dog he'd left behind when he divorced Lanie's mother.

He had an extensive library of classical CDs. Shaunna listened to country and western. It had been playing on both the radio in her house and the ones in her barns. And he could just see her at a business dinner. She'd probably shock his clients with her frankness. She'd certainly shocked him when she talked about castrating the colt she was working with. It was her hand gestures that had gotten to him. Nothing had been left to his imagination. He'd even had the urge to squeeze his knees together.

No, they had nothing in common.

Except, perhaps, a little chemistry.

He grinned and turned onto the highway. Maybe Shaunna had realized that. Maybe she'd told him about castrating that horse as a warning. Well, she didn't have to worry. He wasn't about to start something. Chemistry could be ignored. He'd been doing it for years.

"Just take on the horse," he said to himself, then added, "and Lanie."

Chapter Two

Tyler and his daughter arrived promptly at ten o'clock Saturday morning. Shaunna watched the two of them get out of the car. Tyler was less formally dressed than the first time she'd seen him, his suit replaced by khaki pants, a tan golf shirt and brown loafers. He looked like an ad from *GQ,* and she knew what an hour of working with horses would do to his clothes.

His daughter was more appropriately dressed. The girl had on jeans, a Western-style plaid shirt and cowboy boots. She was as leggy as a colt, thin and pale, and her reddish-brown hair lacked luster. In some ways, Lanie reminded Shaunna of the Mustang they were about to discuss. Both showed the effects of trauma, Lanie's the result of an automobile accident, Magic's caused by the actions of his caretakers.

Lanie limped slightly as she walked toward Shaunna, and Shaunna could see that the girl had a scar on her forehead. It disappeared into the uneven part between her two braids, and considering the stray hairs hanging down the girl's neck, Shaunna guessed that Lanie had braided her own hair.

What she found intriguing was how little the girl resembled her father. Although Shaunna could see that both Lanie and Tyler had blue eyes, the shapes of their faces were entirely different, along with their hair coloring and body builds. Then again, Shaunna knew she resembled her mother far more than she did her father, especially in her eyes.

Besides the differences in their looks, there were other things Shaunna noticed about the pair walking toward her that piqued her curiosity. Father and daughter kept a distance between them, didn't touch and didn't look at each other. Both were staring at her, each with a different expression.

With Lanie, the look was defensive…almost defiant. Her back was rigid, her chin high and her eyes narrowed. Shaunna could tell that the child was measuring her, judging her merit. She looked ready for battle.

Shaunna had seen the look before: in green horses brought to her to be broke; in abused horses that she was asked to salvage; and in the renegades who couldn't be reclaimed. In the first meeting with those horses, they would approach her as the enemy, the predator they should fear. With most, she was able to eliminate those fears and establish communication. With people, she'd learned, that wasn't always possible. She'd never been able to communicate with her mother.

Tyler's look was totally different from his daughter's. His expression showed concern. Silently, he was pleading with her, though Shaunna knew he probably wasn't aware of that. And if she'd been a less scrupulous person, his look would have given her an advantage. He was desperate for her help.

Having seen the Mustang, she understood why.

"Good morning," she said as the two approached.

"Good morning," Tyler responded.

His daughter said nothing, merely narrowed her eyes a shade more.

He stopped a few steps away from Shaunna and glanced down at the girl. "Lanie, this is Ms. Shaunna Lightfeather, the horse trainer I told you about."

"Glad to meet you, Lanie," Shaunna said, and held out her hand.

Lanie ignored the hand and looked at Tyler. "I don't want Magic here," she said. "I want him with me."

"I explained all that to you," Tyler said, giving Shaunna a quick, apologetic glance. "We can't keep a horse where we live."

"We kept a horse where my mother lived," Lanie argued.

"That was different. Your mother lived outside of town. My house is in town, and city ordinances don't allow horses."

"Why can't I live where I used to live?"

Lanie's voice was tense, and Shaunna sensed the girl was close to tears. Tyler softened his tone. "Honey, we've been through this before. That house has been sold."

"I am not your honey," Lanie snapped. "You shouldn't have sold that house. I could've lived there. I could've lived there by myself and taken care of Magic." Her attention switched to Shaunna. "Magic never should have been taken to that stable."

"No, he shouldn't have," Shaunna said in full agreement.

For a moment, Lanie stared at her as if surprised by her response, then the girl looked around, her gaze skimming over the round pen, the two riding arenas, the barns, the paddocks and the house. When she looked back at Shaunna, her attitude was clearly arrogant. "This place is a dump."

"It could use some sprucing up," Shaunna agreed. "You have a couple hundred thousand to give me?"

The girl's eyes merely narrowed again, her chin lifting, and Shaunna knew she hadn't taken the right approach. Working with horses was much easier, but with them, you also had to listen. Lanie was telling her she wasn't happy with the way things were. Problem was, Lanie couldn't go back to the way things had been.

Shaunna tried another tack. "I take it you had a nice place for Magic."

"He was happy there."

I was happy there, Shaunna read in Lanie's body language.

Shaunna looked at Tyler. "If your daughter doesn't want her horse here, it won't work."

"I can't leave him where he is," Tyler said.

"They made him mean," Lanie interjected. "He was never like that before. He loved me." She looked accusingly at her father. "You put him there."

"I didn't know," Tyler said, then looked at Shaunna and repeated the excuse. "I never would have if I'd realized what they would do to him."

She couldn't fault him. He'd already admitted that he didn't know anything about horses. He'd had no idea that the stable he picked had a reputation for abusing horses.

"Have you seen him?" Tyler asked.

She had, and she'd been appalled by what she'd seen. She looked down at Lanie. "What did you think when you saw him?"

"It made me sick."

"Made me sick, too," Shaunna said. "So I brought him here."

"He's here?" The girl's eyes lit up for the first time. "Magic is here?" Then she looked around again and the light went out of her eyes as she screwed up her nose. "In this dump?"

Shaunna ignored the insult and nodded toward the big barn. "He's in there. Last stall on your right." As Lanie started toward the barn, Shaunna called after her, "He's still very upset. Don't go into the stall. Just talk to him from outside."

"He's my horse, and I'll do what I want," Lanie snapped back.

"Even if going in would cause you to lose him?"

Lanie stopped and faced her, and Shaunna knew she had to back up her statement.

"If you go in," she said, "and Magic hurts you, your father will have to call the Bureau of Land Management to come take the horse away. And the way he is now, he'll end up being destroyed. You don't want that, do you?"

"Magic wouldn't hurt me," Lanie said, but Shaunna knew the girl wasn't convinced that was true. She also knew, if Lanie loved her horse, she would do the right thing.

Without answering, Lanie turned around and started walking toward the barn. Shaunna looked at Tyler, and he shook his head. "I'm sorry," he said. "I was afraid she'd be like this. She's so angry about everything."

"She's a lot like her horse, then." Shaunna nodded in Lanie's direction. "I think we'd better follow her in."

"Definitely." Tyler wanted to see the horse again, and he wasn't sure he trusted Lanie to stay out of the stall.

"I hope you don't mind my bringing him here without letting you know," Shaunna said as they walked toward the barn. "I just couldn't leave him there."

"It's hard to believe you got him here." Tyler had been

worried about how they would accomplish that feat. "Last time I saw him, he was ready to eat every human alive."

"It wasn't easy, but we made it."

"Two days ago, you said you didn't have a place for him."

She shrugged. "I moved one of my horses. He'll be fine for a while."

At the entrance to the barn, Shaunna stopped and so did he. From where Tyler stood, he could see Lanie. The girl had already reached the last stall, and to his relief, she was standing on a box outside the stall, looking in.

"This won't work unless she cooperates, you know," Shaunna said, her voice slightly lowered so it wouldn't carry down to Lanie. "If he's going to be her horse, he's got to learn to trust her again. He doesn't know what happened, doesn't know about the accident or that Lanie was hurt. He only knows that he was moved from a place where there was kindness and good care to a hellhole. I'm sure it was traumatic for him to be taken from the wild. Now he's had two experiences where he's been taken from someplace where he was happy. He's learning to distrust all humans, and regaining his trust isn't going to happen overnight. Lanie's got to realize that."

"I'll talk to her," Tyler said although he wasn't sure that would help.

They proceeded down the wide concrete aisle. They were flanked by horse stalls and the smell of horses, along with the smell of fly spray, fresh horse droppings and leather. The only light in the barn came from what filtered in from the open doors at each end and the windows in each stall. He could see fans installed along the ceiling and fluorescent light fixtures, but none of them were on at the moment.

As they neared the last stall, they could hear Lanie talking. "Oh, Magic, what have they done to you?" she kept repeating, and Tyler felt her words stab at his heart.

She was right. He was the one responsible. He'd put the horse in that stable.

He felt Shaunna's hand on his arm, a light and reassuring touch. "You didn't know," she said softly, and he glanced her way.

She was nearly his height, her dark hair pulled back and braided in a single loose braid that hung down to her shoulder blades. Again there was a feather woven into the braid, this time only one, and in the dim light of the barn, her skin tones looked darker.

He'd thought of her often since leaving her. Not that he'd wanted to think about her. Somehow her image just kept popping into his head—memories of how she'd looked, the sound of her voice and the warmth of her smile. Images that had excited him, just as now the touch of her hand and husky sound of her voice had his pulse racing.

"Look at him! He's not any better off here. This place is no better than the other one," Lanie said accusingly, and Tyler's attention returned to his daughter.

"Things may look the same," Shaunna said, her voice calm and soothing as she walked over to stand beside Lanie. "But he's better off here. It's going to take time."

Tyler also moved closer so he could look into the stall. What he saw made him ill.

The horse was standing against the back wall, eyeing them with a wild look. Tyler could see the horse's ribs, their sharp delineation a reminder of the other stable owner's solution for handling ill-tempered horses. What had probably once been a beautiful mahogany coat was now a rough, scruffy, dull red brown, hair missing in some places and in other places so matted with dung they formed hardened clumps. The freeze brand on his neck—his identification as a wild horse—was barely discernible beneath the filth, and his black mane and tail were a twisted, knotted mess. Dirt had turned the white star on his forehead and the white sock on his foreleg a dusty brown, and even at a distance, the smell of him was vile.

The only bit of white that Tyler could see was in the horse's eyes. And it wasn't a good sign.

"All we did yesterday was transport him here and get him settled in the stall," Shaunna said, speaking more to Lanie than to him. "I want him to get used to the smells and sounds around here today, then tomorrow we'll open the door so he can go out." She pointed toward the left side of his stall where the outline of a solid door could be seen. "All of my stalls have direct access to an attached paddock. I felt this stall would be best for your horse since it was built for a stallion. It should hold him."

"He's a gelding," Lanie snapped, looking at Shaunna as if she were stupid.

"I know he's a gelding. He's also a Mustang, and Mustangs, especially those that were born in the wild, are a lot more wily than horses bred in captivity. Until he decides we aren't the enemy, we're going to need something strong to hold him. Otherwise, you're going to be looking all over Bakersfield for your horse."

"He never tried to get out at our place," Lanie said defiantly.

Shaunna didn't lose her composure. "That was then, this is now. At that other stable, he discovered that he could get out. That's why they were keeping him in a stall all the time. We've got to show him that he can't get out."

"I want to touch him, pet him," Lanie said, and stuck her arm through the bars on the stall. "Come here, Magic," she called.

"I wouldn't do that," Shaunna warned.

Lanie glared at her. "He's my horse." Using the flat of her hand, she slapped it against the inside of the stall wall to get the horse's attention. "Magic, come."

The Mustang came.

With a lunge, he sprang toward Lanie, his teeth bared and his ears laid back. The horse's squeal of anger sent a chill down Tyler's spine, and he automatically grabbed Lanie, pulling her off the box and out of danger. The two of them landed on the concrete floor of the aisle, Lanie on top of him. The breath was knocked out of Tyler, but not out of Lanie.

"You ruined him!" she yelled, scrambling to her feet. "Everything's ruined!"

She looked down at Tyler, hatred in her eyes, then turned and ran back down the aisle and out of the barn toward the parking area. Shaunna watched Tyler push himself up from the floor and brush off his khaki slacks. She saw the dirt on the back of his slacks but said nothing. She wanted to know what his reaction was going to be and kept her eyes on his face.

He sighed, shaking his head as he watched his daughter leave the barn. Then he looked at Shaunna. "Well, so much for the horse helping the two of us establish a relationship. I think, if anything, he's driving a bigger wedge between us." Then he added bitterly, "If there could be a bigger wedge."

"She's very angry," Shaunna said, knowing that was an understatement.

"Tell me about it. She acts as if it's my fault that her mother and stepfather are dead. I don't know what to do. Her doctor says she just needs time, but that's what I've been hearing for almost six months, and things haven't been getting any better." Again, he sighed. "I'd better go after her."

"What have you gotten yourself into?" Shaunna muttered to herself as she watched Tyler follow his daughter out of the barn. Then she looked back into the horse's stall.

Magic had returned to the far wall and was watching her, a wary look in his eyes. Given time, she could probably help the horse. She wasn't sure about Tyler and Lanie.

Before they left, Tyler set up an arrangement with Shaunna. Since it was summer vacation and they didn't have to worry about school, every day for the next two weeks Lanie would spend some time at the stable working on reestablishing a relationship with Magic. Someone would bring her, and he would pick her up at night after he got off work. Not only would she spend time with her horse, she would do any chores Shaunna assigned her and take some riding lessons.

Shaunna felt it was the best way for her to see what Lanie could do and how she acted with other horses. The girl was angry, and Shaunna had seen too many people take out their anger on animals. She wasn't about to ask Magic to trust them if Lanie was going to turn around and destroy that trust.

On Monday, Lanie arrived around one o'clock. Shaunna expected the girl to be excited. Instead, she was met with sullen resistance. Even seeing her horse out in the paddock didn't help Lanie's attitude. When the horse didn't come when Lanie called him, it was Shaunna who got the blame. She tried to explain Magic's thinking to the girl, but Lanie wasn't ready to listen.

Shaunna found herself trying to puzzle out the girl as much as the horse, but by Friday, she was ready to give up. The horse was settling in nicely, though it was clear that Magic didn't trust any of them and could still be quite dangerous. Lanie, however, wasn't settling in nicely at all.

No matter what Shaunna said or did, Lanie got angry. Shaunna knew she had a thick hide and could take it—after all, she'd grown up being called incompetent by her father and berated by her mother, but when Lanie started swearing, then decided to take out her anger on one of the other young riders at the stable, Shaunna decided matters had gone far enough. Putting her stable manager in charge, she drove Lanie to her father's place of business.

Tyler was working at his desk, reading over the new tax laws and trying to decide how to summarize them for the benefit of his clients. When his telephone rang, he automatically picked it up.

"There's a woman here who wants to see you," Eve, the firm's receptionist, said. "She has your daughter with her, and they—"

Before Eve finished, his door banged open and Lanie stormed into his office. "She says I can't be around Magic," Lanie shouted. "That I can't even set foot on her property again. Well, I want you to know, I don't care. She's a slave driver, that's what she is!"

Tyler stared at her as she marched up to his desk, then he looked back at Shaunna, who'd followed Lanie into his office. Behind Shaunna was Eve. He nodded toward the receptionist, indicating that he'd like his door closed. Eve discreetly complied while Lanie continued her tirade.

"Look at me!" she cried. "She treats me like dirt!"

Tyler did look at her. Lanie's jeans and boots were filthy, dirt ground into the denim and crusted around her soles. She even had dirt on her face and in her hair, and he had a feeling it wasn't just dirt. The smell in his office was definitely pungent.

"I'm her slave," Lanie said dramatically. "Is this what

you plan on doing with me? Are you going to turn me into a slave?''

Tyler wasn't sure what to think. Lanie's physical condition certainly indicated something was wrong. Though she'd come home dirty the past four days, she'd never been this dirty.

"As for her—" Lanie turned and pointed a finger at Shaunna "—she's not helping Magic. She doesn't do anything with him, just lets him run around in that paddock. She won't even let him into his stall except when it's time for him to eat. And then you know what she makes me do? She makes me clean out his paddock. I have to scoop up his crap.''

She emphasized the word, and Tyler cringed, wondering how far her voice was carrying. He looked at Shaunna, expecting an explanation, but when his gaze met hers, her topaz eyes clear and steady, she merely nodded.

And Lanie wasn't finished. "All she does is order me around. Do this. Do that. Don't do this. Don't do that. I'm supposed to be getting to know my horse, but when do I have time to get to know him? She's got me so damn busy doing other things, I don't have time to get to know him.''

"Don't swear," Tyler said, then spoke to Shaunna. "Is this true?''

"I expect her to follow the barn rules, and I expect her to do what I say when I say it," she said calmly. "And I think she has more to tell you.''

He looked back at Lanie. Immediately, she glared at him. "What does it matter what I tell you? You're going to take her side, aren't you? I should've known it. I'm nothing to you. You don't give a—''

She used the F word, and at exactly that moment, the door to his office swung open. In stormed his boss, Gordon

Fischer, his face a crimson-red, and right behind him was
Gordon's niece, Alicia. Both looked shocked.

As soon as they were in the room, Gordon and Alicia
scanned the office, their expressions almost identical as
their gazes landed on Lanie, then on Shaunna. Both uncle
and niece wrinkled their noses.

Gordon spoke first. "What is going on here?" he demanded, staring directly at Tyler. "Everyone up and down
the hall can hear you two arguing. And the language…"

Tyler mentally cringed. He knew his boss didn't like a
scene. Gordon believed an accounting firm should represent
calm efficiency and traditional values. You did not have
family arguments in your office, and you didn't swear.

Alicia said nothing, but he noticed how she was looking
at Shaunna. The contrast between the two women was even
more apparent than he'd imagined. Alicia was wearing her
red power suit and high heels, her blond hair neatly con-
fined in a twist and her makeup flawless. Shaunna, on the
other hand, wore scuffed cowboy boots, soiled denims, a
faded plaid cotton shirt that had a large stain across the
front, and no makeup at all.

Although Lanie had met Gordon once, the day Tyler had
given her a tour of the offices, and knew Alicia from the
times Alicia had come to the hospital and then to the house,
Tyler thought he'd better introduce Shaunna. "Gordon.
Alicia. I'd like you to meet—"

Lanie didn't let him finish. "Oh great," she snapped.
"Now you're going to be all proper, just like you always
get when Ah-lee-sha is around."

She was looking at Alicia when she stretched out her
name, and Tyler knew Lanie was a ticking time bomb. He
didn't want to imagine what she would come out with next.
"Lanie," he said in warning, hoping she'd get the message.

Lanie glared back at him and let out a series of words

that would make a street kid blush. She then made her departure, bumping against the two standing in her way.

"I never," Alicia said, turning to stare after the ten-year-old.

"Really," Gordon said.

Then Shaunna spoke. "I'm sorry, I shouldn't have bothered you here at work. I'll get her and take her home for you." She headed for the doorway, nodding at Alicia and Gordon as she passed.

Tyler watched her go, too dumbfounded to say anything.

Chapter Three

Alicia looked at Tyler. "Who was that woman?"

"That's Shaunna," he said, not sure if he should also go after Lanie or not. "Shaunna Lightfeather. She's the one who's going to rehabilitate Lanie's horse."

"And what were your daughter and she doing here in your office?" Gordon demanded coldly, his attitude clearly showing his disapproval.

"There was a problem at the stable." Tyler glanced at Alicia and then at her uncle. "I didn't get a full accounting."

"The woman smelled like she'd been rolling in manure." Alicia wrinkled her nose. "And so did your daughter."

There wasn't much he could say about that. "I've discovered that working with horses does leave a smell. Each night, I've been putting Lanie's clothes in the wash as soon as she takes them off."

"You're going to have to do something about that child's

language," Gordon said, shaking his head. "Can't have that kind of talk around here."

"I know." Once again, Tyler wondered if he should go after Lanie.

"Well..." Gordon looked at his niece, then at Tyler. "I'll leave you two alone. But see to it that something like this doesn't happen again, Tyler. It disturbs everyone in the firm."

"I'll talk to Lanie," Tyler said. He watched his boss leave, not sure he liked being reprimanded like a naughty boy.

As Gordon closed the door behind him, Alicia stepped closer to Tyler's desk. "She's very attractive...in a sort of earthy way."

Tyler knew a dangerous situation when he heard one. There was no safe way to respond, so he half lied. "I suppose you could say she's attractive. I really haven't paid that much attention to her looks. I've been more concerned with whether she'll work with Lanie's horse."

"She actually owns the stable where you're boarding the horse?"

"Yes. That is, I think she does." He still wasn't sure what Alicia was getting at.

"Is it a big stable?"

"No, not very big. I'd say she has forty horses there. Maybe fewer. It's nothing fancy." Not a place where Alicia would board a horse...if Alicia had a horse.

She eyed him for a moment, then glanced toward the door as if the image of Shaunna was imbedded there. "You said her last name's Lightfeather? What is that, Navajo or something?"

"I really don't know. Someone said she was part Indian."

"Is she married?"

"No."

Alicia's silence was poignant, and Tyler suddenly realized she was jealous. He found that interesting. Although they'd been dating for nearly a year, he always had the feeling she was keeping him at a distance. But he found that understandable. He was well aware that she was in a social class far above his. And even though he enjoyed her company, most of the events they attended were business oriented. He wasn't looking for love and romance. He'd given up on that years ago. He and Alicia hadn't even slept together.

The one thing he was concentrating on at this point in his life was his career, and Alicia had certainly helped him there. It was at her urging that he'd applied for a position at her uncle's firm, which in turn had led him to the job he now held. And he had to admit she'd been very supportive when he learned about Lanie. Alicia had spend a lot of hours with him at the hospital as he sat by Lanie's side, had talked her uncle into giving Tyler the time off he needed to be with Lanie and had even been offering suggestions on how to handle Lanie now.

Finally, Alicia spoke, her tone clearly cool. "You seem to know quite a bit about this Shaunna woman."

He shook his head. "Only what I found out when I was looking for someone to work with Lanie's horse. I didn't want to move him from one bad situation to another. Shaunna, according to those I spoke with, is the best horse trainer around. Perhaps the best in the country."

There was another moment of silence, Alicia's gaze never leaving his face, then she looked down at her hands and began brushing a fingertip over one of her painted nails. "I think it's commendable," she said, "how much concern you're showing for Lanie and this horse of hers, but you do remember that I don't like horses, don't you? I hope you're not thinking of asking me to accompany you out to that stable or anything?''

"I wouldn't think of it." He could just imagine her re-action if she saw Shaunna's house and the barns. Alicia's condominium was in the best section of town. In fact, her father owned most of the real estate in that area, along with oil wells and other land. Her parents' home, which he'd visited a couple of times, was absolutely palatial. No, she wouldn't think much of Shaunna's stable or house.

Alicia looked back at him and smiled. "I just wanted to be sure we understood each other. Dinner tonight? You could come by my place after work. I have something I'd like to discuss with you. A proposition of sorts."

The bristling gone, Alicia was once again warm and friendly, but Tyler knew that dinner at her place tonight was out of the question. "I'm afraid I can't. I need to find out what exactly happened today. In fact—" he stood "—I think I'd better go make sure Shaunna caught up with Lanie."

Shaunna didn't catch up with Lanie for more than a city block. Where the child thought she was going, Shaunna didn't know, but Lanie was walking with determination, her limp barely discernible. As soon as she reached her side, Shaunna matched her steps to the ten-year-old's. "You showed him, didn't you?" she said as if they'd been carrying on a casual conversation for some time.

Lanie didn't slow her steps and didn't look at her. "Go away."

"Can't."

Lanie did slow, then came to a complete stop. Only when she looked up, could Shaunna see the tears. She wanted to reach out and draw the girl close, but she knew Lanie would only resist. So she stood where she was and looked down at her, waiting for Lanie's next response.

"I hate you," she said.

"I don't hate you."

"I hate everyone."

"So I've noticed."

"I want to ride Magic."

"You can't. Not yet."

Shaunna watched Lanie chew on her lower lip, struggling not to cry. "You're never going to let me ride him," she said, her voice trembling.

"It's not up to me whether you ride him or not. It's up to Magic. We have to give him time to decide that he wants to be ridden. We have to let him know that he can trust us."

"Magic used to trust me. He was sweet and loving before the accident. It's you people who've ruined him."

"Don't include me in that 'you' people. I didn't harm him. You're the one who hasn't shown me that you won't harm him. Look at what happened today. Right there by Magic's paddock, you got into a fight with Bobby."

"He said my horse was ugly."

"So you had to push him into that pile of manure?"

"He pushed me into it, too."

"And that makes it right?"

Lanie stood, glaring at her, her breathing shallow.

Shaunna met her gaze without wavering. "What happens," she asked, "if Magic doesn't do what you want? Do you shove him around? Beat him up?"

Shaunna could tell that the suggestion surprised Lanie. "I wouldn't hurt Magic," she said.

"How do I know that?"

"'Cause I love him."

"Words are cheap." Shauna remembered how many

times her father had said he loved her. Then she'd do something he didn't like, bring home a math paper she'd done poorly on, and he'd hit her.

"I really mean it," Lanie insisted.

"If you love him, then you'll take care of him. You'll give him time to get used to his new surroundings, time to get used to seeing you around. Every time you go into his stall or paddock, you leave your scent. I want him to associate that scent with good things. A clean paddock. Food. Clean water. I want him to see you around the other horses. And I want you watching him, watching how he acts and reacts. I want to know you've got the patience he's going to need. Otherwise, forget it. I am not going to help that horse just to have you turn around and ruin him."

"I won't ruin him," Lanie said defiantly, the tears gone. "I love him."

"And now we've gone full circle. You say you love him. I haven't seen it. Come on." She nodded in the direction her truck was parked. "I'll take you home. You can think about this. If you're willing to do as I ask, then show up tomorrow. If not, have your dad find someplace else for Magic."

Lanie didn't move. "You're not being fair."

"Then what do you think I should do?"

The question seemed to startle the little girl. Lanie stared at Shaunna, then finally answered, "You should let me spend more time talking to Magic."

"Okay. I will." Why not? She'd seen that Lanie knew the basics about horses. She didn't need slave labor, no matter what Lanie thought. And Magic had calmed down enough that he might start responding to Lanie. "Are you ready to go home now?"

Shaunna started heading toward her truck and hoped Lanie would follow. For a moment, she feared she hadn't succeeded, then she heard Lanie's footsteps. The girl walked slightly behind her, but she did go with her toward the truck.

"And I think I should bring him carrots," Lanie said. "He always liked carrots. I used to bring him one every time I went out to see him."

"Okay." Shaunna didn't particularly like feeding horses treats by hand, but if Magic was used to getting them from Lanie, it might help. "Only don't try feeding him by hand right away. Until we're sure he remembers it's you, I don't want to chance his biting your hand off."

"He won't bite my hand off."

Shaunna stopped and looked at the girl, simply lifting her eyebrows and saying nothing.

"Okay," Lanie said, unable to return Shaunna's gaze. "I won't feed him by hand. Not right away. But someday I will."

"Someday," Shaunna agreed, and began walking to her truck again.

Tyler paused at the entrance to the building. Just down the street, he spotted Shaunna and Lanie. Shaunna pulled open the door of a battered blue truck, then glanced back at Lanie. For a moment, the girl stood where she was, then she walked stiff-legged around the front of the truck.

He decided not to call out to them. Shaunna seemed to have the situation under control. She'd said she would take Lanie home. He would call his neighbor and have her keep an eye on Lanie until he got there. By then, maybe he'd have come up with an idea of how to handle this situation.

Shaunna let out a quiet breath of relief when Lanie buckled herself in on the passenger side. "When you first got

Magic," she asked casually as she turned the key in the ignition. "What was he like? What did you do with him?"

As Shaunna drove toward the section of Bakersfield where she knew Tyler lived, Lanie talked, describing how she and her mother had first picked Magic out from all the other Mustangs being offered up for adoption, how they'd trailered him to the barn behind their house and how her mother had had someone come over and break him. Shaunna shook her head, cringing when Lanie went on to tell her how the man had tethered Magic to a post and sacked him out, then tied up one of the horse's hind legs so he couldn't buck when the saddle was put on.

"I don't break horses that way," she said when Lanie was finished. "And I don't train horses that way. I want a horse's cooperation, not his submission."

"My mother said—" Lanie started.

Shaunna interrupted. "We're not talking about your mother, we're talking about me...me, you and Magic." She pulled up in front of the address Tyler had given as his residence when he signed the papers to board Magic at the stable. "This where you live?"

Lanie stared at the house and for a moment said nothing, then she looked back at Shauna, her expression cold. "My mother broke Magic the right way."

"Your mother probably broke Magic the way she knew. A lot of horses have been broken that way. But there are a lot of horse people who now don't think that's the best way, don't believe in forcing a horse into submission. I'm one of those people. We don't think of horses as being stupid and we don't think of them as being the enemy. We believe a horse will be your partner if you let him...and if you understand what he's trying to tell you."

"My mother broke Magic the right way," Lanie repeated defiantly.

Shauna shook her head, unsure of how to get her point across without upsetting Lanie even more. "I don't know what your mother did, or taught you. I only know that I don't believe in punishing a horse if he makes a mistake. If you train a horse that way, he may comply, but he won't really be working with you, and you'll never know when he might rebel. You will always have to be on guard. My way, they do what you want because it's their choice."

"My mother knew more about horses than you'll ever know."

The girl's anger tore at Shaunna, and she wished she knew how to take it away. She remembered herself as a teenager, after she'd run away from home. She'd been that angry, even angrier. She'd been ready to take on the world. The chip on Lanie's shoulder was sawdust compared to the one Shaunna had carried. It was Betsy Helman who had found the patience to blow it away.

"Your mother's gone," Shaunna said softly, knowing the words would hurt. "And Magic needs help. It's your choice. You're the one who has to decide what to do. Think about it tonight. If you don't want to do it my way, have your dad find someone else to work with Magic."

"Yeah, right." Lanie snorted in disgust. "Like he cares what happens to me."

"He cares," Shaunna said, knowing Tyler did. She'd seen him just before they got into the truck, standing near the entrance to his office building, watching them. He cared enough to let Lanie work this out. Shaunna liked that.

Lanie swore, and Shaunna lifted her brows. "That's another thing. I don't allow any swearing around my barn. I don't want to hear any more." Again, Lanie swore, and Shaunna nodded toward the truck door. "It's time for you to go inside. Think about what I've said. You're a smart girl. Very smart. I think you'll make the right decision."

Lanie let loose with another string of swearwords, then pushed open the door and got out. She slammed it shut and headed up the driveway toward the house.

Shaunna saw a woman come out of the house next door and also make for Tyler's place. Lanie looked her way and swore at her. Shaunna shook her head and started her truck again, a backfire reminding her that she needed to get the poor thing into the shop. But to do that, she had to figure out if she had any money in the bank account, and that was the problem.

The sun was setting when Tyler drove into the stable yard. It had taken longer for him to get away from Lanie than he'd expected. Three vehicles were in the parking area, a green van, a red compact, and the blue truck he'd seen Shaunna get into earlier that day. He pulled in next to the van.

His neighbor had agreed to come back and sit with Lanie while he came to the stable to talk to Shaunna. He'd listened to Lanie's side of the story, sprinkled amply with swearwords. Now he wanted to hear Shaunna's version.

He went to the house first. After knocking twice, Maria came to the door and directed him out to the barns. It seemed stable owners didn't work eight hour days. More like daybreak to dark.

Two dogs joined him en route, begging for his attention but never barking. Before he reached the first barn, he noticed a horse and rider in one of the arenas and decided to check it out first. He knew Shaunna gave riding lessons in the evening.

There were three riding rings behind the barns: a small, round pen, a larger, rectangular-shaped arena, and a sizable, show-type arena. The horse and rider he'd seen were in the largest arena, and the moment the rider faced him, he realized it was Shaunna. Stopping where he was, he stood back where he could watch but not be noticed.

From the first time he met her, he'd been aware of a gracefulness in Shaunna's movements. Seeing her on a horse, he was stunned. She wasn't just a rider but a part of the horse. She sat straight in the saddle and moved in unison with every turn and stop the horse made.

The horse spun to the right, then to the left, his hind legs barely moving from one spot, and Tyler shook his head in disbelief as he realized the horse had no bridle or reins. The only sign of any control mechanism was a circle of rope hanging loosely around the horse's neck, but Shaunna's hands weren't on the rope.

The horse dashed forward, then came to a sliding stop, the dust kicking up behind him. Again, there was a turn to the left. Then to the right.

Tyler wasn't sure how, but Shaunna was communicating with the horse. Watching her, he remembered the stories he'd heard when asking around for someone to take on Magic. Each of the stable owners he'd contacted, once they heard of his situation, had told him the one he needed to see was Shaunna Lightfeather. They'd spoken of her with awe, said she could talk to horses and that horses understood her.

Tyler was beginning to believe they were right.

As far as he could tell, however, she wasn't using words. Though she was concentrating on the horse's head, her lips weren't moving. No part of her body seemed to be moving.

"Stick 'em up," a small voice piped up behind him.

Tyler looked away from Shaunna and her horse, then around and down. Behind him stood a little boy about six years old. In his hand was a plastic water gun.

"Jeffery Arnold Prescott!" a woman's voice called sternly from the barn door.

The boy turned away from Tyler and looked toward the barn. So did Tyler. Coming toward them was a woman in her mid-thirties dressed in Western apparel. She held out her hand as she neared.

"What did I say about that gun, Jeffery? Give it to me."

The boy immediately hid the gun behind his back. "I wasn't going to shoot him."

"Give it to me," his mother repeated firmly. For a moment, Tyler didn't think the boy was going to obey, then the hand behind the child's back moved and he held the gun out to his mother. She shook her head at him, then looked at Tyler. "Sorry about that."

"It's okay." After everything else that had happened that day, being held up by a six-year-old seemed appropriate. "I'm discovering kids don't always do as you tell them."

"Tell me about it." Again, she shook her head, then extended her hand to him. "I'm sorry. I'm Chris Prescott. I think I've seen you a couple of times. You've got a daughter, haven't you. Lana or something?"

"Her name is Lanie," he said, and shook Chris's hand. "I'm Tyler Corwin."

"Glad to meet you, Tyler," Chris said. "Shame about that Mustang of yours, but don't you worry. Shaunna will bring him around. She can do anything with a horse." She looked beyond Tyler. "Can't you, Shaunna?"

"We'll see," Shaunna said from a spot nearby, and Tyler turned to find she'd left the arena and was now sitting on her horse only a few feet away.

The horse was blowing slightly and a sheen of sweat covered his mahogany-brown body. He still had no bridle, only one of the fly masks that all of the horses wore. And Shaunna still wasn't touching him, yet the horse stood where he was, only occasionally stomping a foot or switching its tail at an insect.

"Jeffery and I are leaving now," Chris said. "Time for both of us to hit the sack. I put Flash back out in the pasture."

"How'd he go for you tonight?" Shaunna asked, slapping at one of the flies that had landed on her horse's neck.

"Great. I tried that trick you showed me for changing leads, and it worked. He's really getting it now."

"I had a great ride, too," Jeffery said, looking up at Shaunna.

"Did you now?" she said. "Well, I'm glad to hear that. Did Mischief do what he was supposed to do?" With barely any effort, Shaunna swung her leg over her horse's back and slid off. Only then did she take hold of the rope around the horse's neck.

"He got into mischief," Jeffery answered.

"Guess that's how he got his name."

"Guess so." Jeffery giggled, and Tyler had a feeling this was an ongoing conversation between Shaunna and the boy.

"We'll see you tomorrow," Chris said, then held out a hand to her son. "Come on Jeffery. Time for a hot bath."

"See you tomorrow," Jeffery echoed, going with his mother.

Shaunna watched them for a moment, then looked at Tyler and smiled. "I've been expecting you."

Chapter Four

"I thought I'd come hear your side of the story," Tyler said.

"Fair enough." Shaunna ran a hand along her horse's neck and secured the rope so it wouldn't slip down over his head. "ChiChi's hot. Do you mind if we walk around in the arena while we talk?"

Tyler glanced at the dusty arena, down at his loafers and tan slacks, then back at her. "Fine with me."

"You're going to have to start wearing grubbies out here." Anything to make him stop looking so good. Although she'd been expecting him, she hadn't expected her heart to skid to a stop when she saw him by the barn talking to Chris and her son. Runaway cattle couldn't have stirred her stomach more than the sight of Tyler did. It took all of the self-control she possessed to act casual as she walked beside him back toward the arena.

Her horse followed her as she knew he would. Tyler was the one she wasn't sure how to read. Was he angry? About to tell her that Magic wouldn't be there much longer?

Horses were much easier to read than people. Horses didn't set her hormones racing.

"So what did Lanie tell you?" she asked, expecting just about anything from the girl.

"That you said Magic had to go."

"That wasn't exactly what I said." Though it was probably what she should say—for her own sake at least. "I told her it was her choice. If he stayed, she had to follow my rules. If she couldn't do that, he had to go."

As she walked slowly around the arena, her horse following, Tyler matched her steps, staying on her left. He was so close she could hear him take in a deep breath and slowly release it. She still wasn't sure how he was going to respond and didn't say a word, her mind bouncing from an awareness of him as a man to a concern for his daughter and her horse.

At last, he did say something. "You've given her a choice, but there's nowhere else for the horse to go. Before I came to you, I talked to several stable owners. No one wanted him. Not the way he is now. They all said the person I should talk to was you. So if Magic goes anywhere, it will be back to the Bureau of Land Management. And from there, probably to slaughter."

Which she didn't want happening. "Does Lanie understand the consequences if she doesn't leave him here?"

"I've told her." He shook his head. "I don't know. She's so angry I'm not sure she's thinking straight."

"What was she like before the accident? Before her mother and stepfather died?"

"Before the accident?" he repeated, then went silent.

She could tell from his body language that her question had made him uneasy. She didn't push. She was beginning to discover he was a man who thought before he answered.

She liked that. He also seemed to listen. That in itself was a rare quality.

Finally, he did respond. "To be honest," he said, "I really don't know what she was like. Before the accident, I had no contact with her. Until the night the police called and said my ex-wife was dead and Lanie was in the hospital fighting for her life, I hadn't seen her since she was six months old."

Stunned, Shaunna stopped walking and so did her horse. That wasn't the answer she expected. "You hadn't seen your daughter in nine years?"

He glanced her way, then straight ahead. "There were extenuating circumstances."

ChiChi nudged her shoulder, and Shaunna remembered she had to keep him moving. She gave the horse a pat and started walking again, but that didn't stop her from grilling Tyler. "What kind of extenuating circumstances? Did your ex have a restraining order against you or something?"

"No, nothing like that. I wouldn't have gotten custody of Lanie if there'd been that sort of problem."

She was glad to hear that. But if Tyler hadn't done anything wrong, it meant he'd done the same thing her father had. "In other words, you divorced your wife and walked away from your daughter. How could you do that?"

"As I said, there were extenuating circumstances. Lanie..." He looked up at the sky, stars already visible in the dimming light, then back at her. "I'm sorry. I—I really don't feel I can talk about this."

"Can't talk about it? You desert your child and you can't talk about it? Gads, you men." She would never understand them.

"All I can say is that my decision to totally separate my life from Lanie's wasn't due to anything I'd done. In fact, for those six months before Barbara and I split up, I adored that little baby. It's…it's just something that happened, something I have to deal with personally."

She'd just bet he had to deal with it personally. And so did Lanie. No wonder the girl was angry. Shaunna knew the feeling well.

But since Tyler's desertion of his daughter wasn't anything that could be changed, she decided to focus on the problem at hand. "So you basically know nothing about Lanie other than what you've learned since the accident. Is that right?"

"Pretty much so."

"What about her grandparents on your ex-wife's side?"

"Dead. And George's parents live in North Carolina and rarely saw her. There are some health problems with them, I think."

"And your ex never had any more children?"

"No. And I don't know why not. That is, I don't know if they didn't want more or couldn't have more. Once the divorce was final, I basically severed all contact with Barbara."

And with his daughter. No matter what the circumstances, Shaunna still found that difficult to swallow.

She liked Tyler. No, that wasn't exactly true. She had thought she liked him, but now that she knew he'd deserted his daughter, she had a different opinion of him. All she had to do was convince her body that she didn't find him attractive. Find a way to stop the quivery feelings she got around him. She didn't want him raising her blood pressure. Didn't want to be turned on by him. It just happened. And that irritated her.

She'd thought she was past those days when a man's smile or touch would excite her. No man had aroused a sexual desire in her for a long time. Which had been just fine with her. Why subject yourself to heartache? That was her philosophy.

She had been abandoned three times in her twenty-eight years: by her father, then Dale and finally that sleazy accountant she'd thought was her friend. Four times, if you counted the way her mother had treated her. And five if you counted Betsy's death as abandonment. As far as Shaunna was concerned, only a fool would set herself up to be deserted again. And Tyler had already shown he could abandon someone he professed to love.

Once again she stopped. This time she felt ChiChi's neck and girth and decided he was cool enough to put up. "I'm going to take him into the barn and untack him," she told Tyler, and headed toward the big barn. "Come along. We still need to decide on a plan of action with Lanie."

Tyler agreed. He wished he could tell her more about Lanie, explain the circumstances that had led him to walk away from the baby he'd loved. In retrospect, it had been a mistake, but at the time his decision seemed right. To talk about it now, especially to a virtual stranger, would only jeopardize the relationship, as tenuous as it was, that he had with Lanie.

He watched Shaunna walk ahead, her horse following close behind, occasionally giving her a nudge. Oddly enough, even though he'd only known her a short while, he didn't really feel she was a stranger. He wanted her understanding—and her approval—and that realization left him uneasy.

"I probably shouldn't have brought Lanie to your office," she said, glancing back at him. "If I'd known how she would act, I wouldn't have, but I thought it was something we should deal with immediately. I hope I didn't cause any problems. I take it that was your boss who came into your office. Or your bosses."

"One boss, one boss's niece."

Shaunna stopped halfway down the aisle in the barn and took off the rope looped around her horse's neck. "Ah, the boss's niece," she repeated, and smiled. "Lanie's mentioned her."

"Not in the most flattering terms, I'm sure. She doesn't seem to like Alicia."

"Your daughter doesn't seem to like anyone right now. How's this Alicia feel about her?"

"She thinks I'm being too lenient with Lanie, that I need to discipline her more."

Shaunna pulled the saddle off the horse, taking a step back as she did. The saddle looked heavy, and he felt he should do something to help. Stepping closer, he reached out to grab hold of it.

His fingers touched hers. Just barely…and just for a second.

Shaunna stopped moving, her gaze meeting his, and he knew he should have kept his hands to himself. In that touch—in that second—an awareness had passed between them. It was like discovering you held the winning lottery ticket. Like taking a step into thin air. Exciting and heart-stopping. Earth-shattering.

Shaken, he drew his hands back and moved away. She said nothing, but in her eyes he saw the same confusion…and desire he was experiencing. She continued putting the saddle up as if nothing had happened, but he knew something had. Rational or not, there was an attraction between them.

She didn't look at him as she sponged off the sweat marks on her horse's back and neck. She didn't even glance his way when she finally spoke. "She's very beautiful. The boss's niece, I mean."

Shaunna's voice was huskier than usual, hesitant. Tyler

wondered what his voice was going to sound like. He gave it a try. "She said the same thing about you."

Shaunna faced him. "You're kidding."

"No." He remembered Alicia's comment clearly. "She said you were very attractive in an earthy sort of way." And he agreed. Especially at the moment. With a slight blush highlighting her swarthy coloring, Shaunna was too damned attractive.

"Right." She turned to her horse again, using a squeegee to remove the excess water from his coat. "By earthy, she probably meant I was dirt. Both she and your boss looked at me as if I were scum."

"It was the horse smell," he defended. "It was rather strong."

"Yeah." She didn't sound convinced.

The squeegee went back into the bucket, and Shaunna gave her horse a pat, then started out of the barn. Tyler realized she was leaving and he'd better follow.

"Speaking of the smell," Shaunna said once they were outside, "did Lanie ever tell you what happened?"

"She said a boy pushed her into a manure pile."

"Did she mention why?"

"She said he's a bully."

Shaunna opened the gate to a paddock and gave her horse a loving pat on the haunches. Without a glance her way, the horse trotted in, heading for his feed. Once the gate was latched again, she faced Tyler. "Bobby is about Lanie's age. He's a pest and totally insensitive, but he's hardly a bully. He called her horse ugly and she jumped on him, pushing him into the pile of manure she'd raked out of Magic's paddock. He then tripped her up, so she also fell into it."

"You saw this?" Shaunna's story definitely didn't match Lanie's.

"I saw it. That's when I decided to step in and when she decided to give me a taste of her colorful language. At that point, I felt you needed to be involved."

"She didn't learn that language from me." Though he was known to toss out an occasional damn and hell, he didn't normally swear. He hadn't heard some of the words Lanie used earlier since he'd been in the navy. "In fact, I've been wondering where she did learn it. Barbara didn't swear when we were married. It either had to be from George or her school friends."

"Seeing your expression when she started swearing in your office," Shaunna said, "I knew it wasn't something you'd taught her. So how long has she been doing it?"

"Just the past couple of weeks. It seems to be getting worse every day."

"Probably because she knows it bothers you." Shaunna started back toward the barn. "I just have to turn out a couple of lights, then I'm through here. Do you want to come up to the house and have some lemonade or iced tea?"

"Sounds good." Actually, a stiff drink sounded better. Coping with a ten-year-old, he was beginning to discover, could drive a man to drink. Coping with these crazy emotions Shaunna aroused could also drive a man to drink, though he certainly didn't intend to turn to alcohol for answers.

"She's going to test you." Shaunna slowed her steps so she was walking beside him. "Just as Magic is going to test us when we start working with him. Things have happened that they don't understand, and they're in new surroundings. They want to know their boundaries, want to know what's going to happen if they do something."

Shaunna gave a quick glance around the barn, looking for anything out of place. The sounds of horses shifting weight in their stalls, stomping off flies and chewing their food was reassuring. All appeared to be fine. After flicking the light switch, she headed for the house.

Tyler walked beside her. Again, he was silent. This time, it bothered her. She'd expected a response to her comment about Lanie, either agreement or disagreement. Finally, she couldn't restrain herself and glanced his way.

He was looking at her, his smile as warm as a summer morning and way too sensuous. Quickly, she looked ahead again. The quivering sensation was back in her stomach and totally unwelcomed. "What?" she asked, wishing she knew when she'd lost control of her emotions.

"What do you mean 'what?'"

She knew he was laughing at her reaction and was glad it was dark out. Even so, she feared he'd seen the flush of color on her cheeks. This definitely wasn't like her. She didn't blush and she didn't get flustered. She didn't give a damn about men—normally.

Except, in the barn, when his hand touched hers, she'd gotten flustered. Some people called the reaction chemistry. She called it annoying. From the first time she met him, Tyler had been confusing her emotions. It had to stop.

"What are you looking at?" she asked, the heat of his gaze unrelenting.

"You," he said softly. "I like the way you think. You put things in perspective."

All too clearly, she knew she had to put her reactions in perspective. *Keep your mind on Lanie,* she told herself. *Don't think about Tyler. Think about his daughter.* The daughter he'd deserted for so many years.

"She needs your help," she said, aware there was a slight quaver to her voice.

"But how do I help her?" he asked. "That's the question."

Shaunna opened the screen door and motioned for him to enter the house first. She kicked off her boots in what was her boot room, laundry room and general storage area, then followed him into the kitchen, snapping on the light as she entered. With a motion of her hand, she indicated a chair he could use, then she went into the living room. Maria was sitting in the easy chair, snoring softly. The television was on, but Shaunna decided not to wake her. She could check the refrigerator herself. Either Maria had made some iced tea or lemonade, or she hadn't.

She found a pitcher on the top shelf, gave it a sniff, then turned to Tyler. "Lemonade all right?"

"Fine."

He was looking at her again, watching her with those warm blue eyes of his. She didn't want to know what he was thinking. She didn't want to start drowning in those oceans of blue. Quickly, she brought up a subject she was sure would ground her. "Lanie said you've been dating Alicia for some time."

"About a year now, off and on."

"I take it, then, that it's serious." She hoped so. That would eliminate all the problems. She absolutely never, ever, went after another woman's man.

"I suppose that depends on your definition of serious. I haven't dated anyone else during that time, and I do like her, but up until today, I would've said we were just friends. Today, I realized she was jealous of you."

"Jealous of me?" Shaunna retrieved two glasses from the cupboard. "Now there's a laugh."

"Why? You're an attractive woman. And don't deny knowing that. You must have looked into a mirror sometime in your life."

"And saw a nose that's too broad, a face that's too square and weird-colored eyes."

"Beautiful eyes."

The way he was looking at her, she almost believed him. Almost.

"What about you?" he asked. "Anyone serious in your life?"

She supposed she could lie and say yes, but the truth seemed as good. "Hardly. Keeping up this stable takes all of my time and energy. Sometimes I'm not sure if Betsy was being kind or not when she turned this place over to me." Shaunna finished pouring the lemonade and got some ice.

"Betsy?"

"Betsy Helman—the woman who originally owned this place. Wonderful woman."

She carried the two glasses to the table, setting one in front of him and the other on the opposite side of the table...as far as she could get from him. She needed the distance. And the breathing space.

"Betsy taught me everything I know about horses...and about life. One thing she always emphasized was that life is full of choices—choices with consequences. I've given Lanie a choice, Tyler. You need to explain exactly what will happen to Magic if she chooses not to follow my rules. It must be her decision, but you must be willing to follow through if she's determined not to clean up her language and follow my orders. The horse will have to go."

"You'd have me send him back?" He looked surprised by the suggestion.

Yes was the answer called for, but to sacrifice Magic to teach Lanie a lesson seemed too cruel. The horse wasn't to blame for what had happened. She couldn't condemn him because mankind had been less than "kind" to him. "No, I would hope you wouldn't send him back," she said on a sigh. "You and I will just have to work something out if it comes to that."

Tyler leaned back in his chair, not quite sure how to explain the feeling of happiness welling inside him. Perhaps it was because he hadn't wanted to think of the horse ending up as dog food. Or perhaps it was because Shaunna's answer had shown she was a caring person. He grinned. "You're a sucker."

"I am not. I just—"

"You're a sucker," he repeated. "And that's why you have all these horses and dogs and cats around. You care. You care about Magic, and you care about Lanie." And though it wasn't an economically sound way to do business, he liked it. "That's nice."

"Yeah, real nice." She sighed and looked at the pile of bills beside her, tapping the top one with a fingertip. "Now what would be really nice is if these feed suppliers would stop sending me these bills."

Tyler watched her push the pile even farther to the side, then reach for her glass of lemonade. Her hand was halfway to the glass when some of the papers slid off the top of the stack and dropped to the floor. They made a noise, and she looked in that direction. Just a glance. Just enough so that instead of wrapping her fingers around the glass, her hand hit its edge.

It all happened before he could move. In an instant, the glass tipped over, lemonade spilling across the table. The glass rolled toward the edge. Shaunna grabbed for it, then he grabbed for it, but neither of them was quick enough. With a crash, the glass hit the linoleum, splintering into pieces.

"Damn!" she said, pushing her chair back and standing.

"Don't move," he ordered, remembering she didn't have any boots on. "There's glass everywhere."

She did move, but only to kneel so she could start picking up the shards that were closest to her chair and feet. "Maria's in the other room. She was sleeping when I looked. If you'll—"

"No need to wake her," Tyler said, looking around the kitchen. "Do you have a broom or something?"

"There's a broom and a dustpan in the closet over there." Shaunna pointed toward a narrow door to her left.

He found the broom and dustpan, along with a mop. Quickly, he swept up the glass and mopped the lemonade off the linoleum, though the floor still felt sticky as he walked across it.

By the time he'd finished, Shaunna was sitting again. She shook her head as he came back toward the table. "It's been one of those days."

"I know what you mean." In the past few hours, he'd been reprimanded by his boss, gotten into another battle with Lanie and couldn't understand why he was fascinated by a woman so totally his opposite. "Come on, let's get those wet socks off. They're soaked with lemonade."

She looked down at her feet as if she'd totally forgotten her socks, then leaned over to pull one off. Suddenly, her head was close to his, her mouth only inches away. After that, he couldn't really explain what happened.

When he'd come to the stable, he hadn't planned on kissing her. Not even when he'd entered her house. Not until she leaned close did the thought occur to him, and then, before he knew it, he was looping his arm around the back of her neck and drawing her head closer. And even then, he didn't really think about what he was doing. He simply reacted, his mouth touching hers.

He'd kissed so many women in his thirty-four years, he didn't expect anything special. Kisses were kisses, he'd decided long ago. Some were wet and mushy. Some hard and punishing. Lips touching lips. A physical expression of a hormonal urge. Nothing more.

At that moment, he realized how wrong he'd been. Oh, how very wrong. There were kisses, and then there were *kisses*. Ones that hit you like a punch in the gut, exploded in your head, ricocheted through your body until your toes curled and shattered all sensibility. Ones that made you do things you never thought you would do.

He wasn't even aware he'd stood, bringing Shaunna to her feet with him. Not once did he lose contact with her mouth, only with reality. And when he drew her close, he was amazed by how well her body fitted with his, how softly her curves melded against his angles.

His body was hard. Painfully so. And it didn't make any sense. For a year, he'd been dating one of the richest, most beautiful women in Bakersfield, and not once had he stepped out of line or been tempted to go beyond the limits Alicia set. Control was his middle name. Control had gotten him through his divorce with Barbara, had allowed him to walk away from Lanie. Control gave order to his life.

He was out of control.

Chapter Five

Shaunna knew she had to stop kissing Tyler Corwin, had to stop combing her fingers through his hair, mussing it and feeling its vibrant texture. And she would stop, just as soon as the wonderful sensations spiraling through her went away and she could think.

Deep down, she knew kissing Tyler was crazy. It was totally wrong. She didn't want to get involved with any man. Kissing led to trouble, got emotions stirred that should be left dormant.

Problem was, kissing Tyler felt too damned good to stop. It got the blood pumping and nerve endings jangling. Kissing Tyler made her forget everything except for the feel of his hands.

And those hands were everywhere, sifting through her hair, stroking her shoulders and back and pulling her hips up against his. There was no doubting his reaction to kissing her. She could feel his arousal. Just as she was sure he could feel how swollen her breasts had become. That had to be why he was pulling at her shirt, drawing it up from the waist of her jeans. Her nipples ached for his touch, and so did another part of her body, lower and deeper.

It was crazy. Here she was, kissing a man in her kitchen and thinking of making love with him. She didn't do things like that. She couldn't even remember the last time she'd been with a man. Making love wasn't something she took lightly. She had to be in love to make love, and she wasn't falling in love, never again.

"No," she said, surprised by how faint her voice sounded. How weak and indecisive.

She wasn't weak, and she wasn't indecisive. She knew who she was, where she'd been and where she didn't want to go. She knew her strong points and her weaknesses. And she certainly didn't want to get involved with a man who'd deserted his child.

"No," she said again, more strongly this time. Pushing her palms against his chest, she drew back.

He stopped pulling at her shirt and looked at her. In his eyes, she saw desire. It was up to her, she knew. Give in, and they would both lose control.

"No," she said one more time and sucked in a deep breath.

She wasn't afraid. Somehow she knew he wouldn't go beyond her limits. It was setting those limits that was giving her trouble. Reason demanded one thing. Her body was begging for something else.

As she watched his face, she knew when reason returned to him. He closed his eyes and released his hold on her. When he looked at her again, guilt had replaced desire. "I'm—I'm sorry," he said. "I don't usually... I shouldn't have... You..." He motioned toward her chair. "And I..." With a sweep of his hand, he gestured toward the floor, and she understood.

"It happened. Just forget it." There was nothing more

to say. They'd gotten close, and that was their mistake. The chemistry had been there from the start. Ignoring it hadn't made it go away. But they had to ignore it.

Not that she thought they would forget what just happened, but they had to pretend they had if they were going to work together to help Lanie and Magic. They had to pretend there was no attraction, no physical desire. It was best for everyone.

Or so she told herself.

She stepped back so she could move without fear of bumping into him, then stripped off her socks in two quick motions.

"I think I'd better go," Tyler said, taking a step back himself. "I'll—I'll talk to Lanie in the morning. Since it's Saturday, I don't have to go to work. I'll give her the choices, make it sound as though Magic will have to go if she doesn't clean up her act, then let her decide. We'll either show up sometime in the morning or I'll give you a call."

Shaunna nodded. It was all they could do for now. Let Lanie decide. "Tell her you talked to me tonight and convinced me to let her ride tomorrow. I was going to let her anyway, but she might as well think you got me to agree to it. Tell her it'll be one of the stable horses so I can see how she rides."

He nodded. "Sounds good. I'll be the good guy."

"And I'll be the bad guy. Why not? As long as it works."

Saturday morning, Shaunna gave her usual lessons, the riders ranging in age from six to sixty and their riding skills ranging from green novice to expert. She tried not to think of Tyler and Lanie, but every time a car pulled into the yard, she looked. And every time the telephone rang, she cringed, waiting to hear Maria or Todd, her stable manager, call out her name.

Tyler didn't call, and it was nearly noon before father and daughter arrived. Shaunna sighed in relief when she noted Lanie seated beside him. As they got out of the car, Shaunna made a point of concentrating on the students riding around her in the midsize arena; nevertheless, she saw Lanie go toward Magic's paddock, a bunch of carrots in her hand. Shaunna hoped Tyler kept a close eye on Lanie.

Magic had calmed down considerably in the past seven days, especially now that he'd gone through the testing stages and discovered he couldn't get out of the paddock and wasn't going to be locked in his stall for more than a few hours. Shaunna was pleased with his progress, but she wasn't sure how he'd react to a hand holding carrots. Hands, the horse had learned, held whips and clubs. Hands meant pain, not pleasure.

As soon as she could, Shaunna brought the class in the arena to an end. "Cool your horses off. Tell them what a good job they did," she told the riders.

Once she saw the horses stretch out their necks and relax, she knew all would be calm. She could leave them, at least for a while, and check on Lanie.

Tyler saw Shaunna coming toward them. Instantly, he remembered the night before. How soft she'd felt in his arms. How warm and alive. The memory heated his body, bringing an immediate reaction. Not one he wanted. All night he'd tried to understand what had happened in Shaunna's kitchen. It made no sense. If he was going to get hot and bothered, why not with Alicia? Why pick someone so totally his opposite when he was already dating someone? What insanity had overtaken him in that kitchen?

He didn't want emotional chaos. He was a debits-and-credits man, everything orderly. No getting off balance.

He glanced down at Lanie. She'd been holding out a carrot, cajoling Magic to come get it for five minutes. Magic was still standing in the middle of the paddock, eyeing her suspiciously. Defiantly, Lanie looked at Shaunna. "He won't come."

"But he's watching you, listening to you. That's good. See how his ears are flicked toward you."

Lanie looked at the horse, then frowned. "But he won't come any closer. He came that close, then stopped, and he won't come any closer."

"At least he didn't lunge at you and isn't trying to attack you. That's closer than he's come to anyone else on his own."

"Really?" Again, Lanie glanced at Shaunna.

"Really. I haven't been able to get him even that close."

"He loves me," Lanie said. "That's why he came closer."

"He's remembering," Shaunna said. "You just have to give him time." She motioned toward the carrot in Lanie's hand. "Put that down just inside the fence, then leave. We'll all leave. That will give him a chance to come over and sniff the carrot. My guess is he'll eat it, then when you come back, I bet he'll move even closer. And if you keep trying, after a while he'll probably come all the way because he'll remember that you were nice to him. All it takes is time."

Lanie looked at the carrot in her hand, then at her horse. Finally, she put the carrot down on the ground just inside the paddock and stepped away, toward Shaunna. "Tyler said I could ride today."

Tyler noted she still didn't call him Dad or "Father," and that she offered the statement as a challenge, defying

Shaunna to disagree. He looked at Shaunna and saw her smile.

"He convinced me you'd be able to handle it, so we'll give it a try. You take care of Magic's stall and water, then as soon as I'm finished with the class in the arena, I'll saddle up Bangs. You can ride him in my one o'clock class."

Tyler stood by the fence, watching the five horses and their riders circle the arena, Shaunna standing in the middle. He could understand why her skin was bronzed. Though the temperature was cooler than normal for a day in June, the sun was out, and the cowboy hats Shaunna and all of her students were wearing couldn't completely shield their skin. Even with the sunscreen he was using on Lanie, he'd noticed she'd picked up a bit of a tan in the past week. The color was wiping out the sickly paleness from her hospital stay and the hours she'd spent in her room, refusing to do anything. He was beginning to think her doctor was right— the horse would help her to recover.

And he was pleased to see she could ride a horse. At least, she was staying on and not bouncing all over the place, which was more than he'd ever accomplished. Lanie even smiled when Shaunna singled her out, complimenting her on the nice touch she had on the reins and telling the other four in the class to notice how she wasn't jerking on the horse's mouth. The woman should be a psychologist.

The more he watched Shaunna, the more entrancing he found her. She might not be a good businesswoman—the pile of bills on her kitchen table was growing rather than shrinking—but she definitely had a way with horses. He'd seen how they acted around her. There were the nuzzles and the nudges, all responded to with a touch of her own, whether a pat or a stroke. She didn't seem to mind if one slobbered on her shoulder or rubbed a sweaty neck against her arm, and he could understand why she didn't wear fancy clothing. Denims, boots and cotton shirts were her wont, most of them faded, scuffed or torn.

She was a total contrast to Alicia, who had a fit if she chipped a fingernail and admitted to spending way too much on clothes. She'd once told him that to look good, you needed to buy the best.

Tyler stared at Shaunna.

She looked good to him. Tall and willowy. Natural and unassuming. Once again, he found his body responding and looked away.

This was not good. To be honest, it was totally ridiculous. He had nothing in common with Shaunna other than she was Lanie's riding instructor and Magic's hope for survival. He knew nothing about horses. She obviously knew nothing about accounting.

She made him lose control.

He didn't like that.

Drawing in a deep breath, he tried to clear his mind. Funny, the one thing he liked about Alicia was her sensible way of looking at life. She didn't do things on impulse. She was in control. And when he was around her, he was in control.

He blew out another breath.

Controlling that kiss last night had been impossible. He hadn't thought, he'd acted—then reacted. In seconds, he'd been on fire. But fire burned. Left scars. He'd been burned by Barbara, burned badly. He'd loved her, had thought she loved him. And then he'd discovered the truth.

But never again. No more playing with fire. No more allowing himself to fall in love. He would resist the sparks, would keep his distance from Shaunna. He could do it.

* * *

Shaunna was pleased with the way Lanie rode. The child had a natural balance and was kind to her horse's mouth. Too often young riders tried to use the reins to keep their balance, the result being a lot of jerking on the bit. Bangs was used to that, had endured the jerks and pulls of many a young rider and some older ones, too. Shaunna was sure he was enjoying his outing this morning more than some he'd tolerated.

And then Lanie got angry.

"No," the girl yelled, and jerked viciously on the reins, pulling her horse to the left.

"What's the matter?" Shaunna called to her.

"He's twitching."

"He's trying to get a horsefly off."

"Well, I don't like it."

"So should I jerk your mouth around if you do something I don't like?"

"You jerk me around as it is." Lanie stopped her horse in the middle of the arena and dismounted, glaring at Shaunna. "I want to ride Magic. I don't want to ride one of your dumb horses with a lot of other dumb people."

Lanie glared at the other four riders in the arena, but so far, Shaunna noticed, Lanie hadn't used any swearwords.

"I'm out of here," the girl said, walking away from her horse.

"If you're finished riding, fine," Shaunna said firmly, not moving from where she stood. "But you don't leave until you've taken care of your horse. And don't you dare abuse him."

Lanie stopped halfway to the gate and looked at her. "I don't have to."

"You don't have to do anything, but there are consequences." She hoped Lanie got the message.

For a moment, the girl said nothing, then she stomped

back to her horse and grabbed the reins. Shaunna feared she would jerk on them when she saw Lanie's hand begin to move sharply, but then the girl stopped herself. After giving Shaunna a look, she stepped forward, dragging more than leading the horse, but not actually jerking on his reins.

Tyler opened the gate for her, looking at Shaunna as he did. She nodded, okaying the procedure. It was better to have Lanie and the horse out of the arena than to force the child to stay. It would also give Tyler a chance to talk to Lanie and hopefully convince her that her behavior was wrong.

Watching father and daughter walk back to the barn, Bangs now following willingly, Shaunna wondered if they would ever get through to the child. Lanie's blowup had been totally unexpected and totally without reason. It was as if Lanie suddenly realized she was being nice and had to do something quite the opposite.

"What do you want us to do?" one of the other riders asked, bringing Shaunna's attention back to the class.

"Do some figure eights," she said, and slapped her side. "I want to see how close you can get to me."

"I want to go home," Lanie said.

"Don't we have to do something with him?" Tyler stared at the horse Lanie had been riding, not sure what to do.

"He's her horse. Let her take care of him."

"But you were riding him."

"I want to ride Magic."

"Lanie, we've been over this before." He looked down the aisle, toward Magic's stall. "You can't even get him to come close to you. How are you going to ride him?"

"You hate me, don't you? I'm just a burden. You all hate me."

"Lanie." He saw the tears in her eyes and quickly knelt down, drawing her into his embrace. "I don't hate you, and you're not a burden. I love you."

She pulled free. "You don't love me. You just have to take care of me."

"That's not true."

"Oh, yeah? Alicia said I was an incontinence."

"She said what?" He had no idea what Alicia might have said to Lanie, but he doubted it was anything about incontinency.

"An incontinence. You know, a problem. Something that gets in the way of your plans. She said it one day when she came over to the house. And it's true, isn't it? You didn't have a kid, and now you do."

"It's true that I didn't have you before and now I do, but you're not an *inconvenience,* and I'm not taking care of you just because I have to. I'm doing it because I want to, because I care about you and love you."

For a moment, Lanie said nothing, only looked at him, and he thought maybe he'd gotten through to her. Then she glared at him. "Is that why you want to send me away to a private school?"

"Who said I wanted to do that?"

"Alicia did. And you do anything Alicia says."

He stood, dusting dirt from his slacks. "I didn't realize you overheard us talking about that. Lanie, we were just discussing the idea. Alicia thinks a private school would help you catch up on what you missed last year. She went to one, you know."

"La-di-da." Lanie made a face.

"She also said you'd learn some manners there. And she's probably right."

"See? You are sending me away."

Looking at Lanie, so belligerent, he wondered if there

was anything he could say that would make any difference. She sure wasn't making loving her easy.

According to Shaunna's philosophy, what he needed to do now was give Lanie a choice. He was willing to try. "I think the decision to go to a private school or not should be yours."

"Mine?" Lanie looked at him warily. "You'd let me decide if I wanted to go or not?"

"Yes. Alicia said it's an excellent school and that you could come home weekends. Before the summer's over, we'll take you there and let you look it over. If you decide you want to go, that would be fine. If you decide you don't want to go, that would also be fine." He could live with either decision she made. She was a bright girl. No matter which school she attended, she would catch up on her work. He was sure of that.

"You really wouldn't make me go if I said I didn't want to?"

"Really." She didn't look completely convinced, but he noticed a softening in her eyes. Tyler felt that was a step in itself and decided to change the subject. "Now, why don't you show me how to take a saddle and bridle off and put a horse up. Then we'll see if we can get Magic to come closer for a carrot."

Although Shaunna kept her distance, she was aware of what Lanie and Tyler did that afternoon. She watched Lanie try to coax Magic closer, and by midafternoon, Lanie had enticed the Mustang a few feet more. Still, the horse didn't come all the way to the fence, not until after Lanie left the carrot in his paddock and walked away.

Tyler stayed with his daughter, and Shaunna used him as a means of getting Lanie to do things. "Show your dad how to clean tack," she said, pausing before going out on a trail ride with three of her boarders. "That saddle you brought over needs to be cleaned. There's some saddle soap and oil in the tack room that you can use, along with rags and silver polish."

She left it at that and rode off, the three boarders joining her. When she returned, she saw father and daughter sitting just inside the barn, near Magic's stall, busily cleaning Lanie's bridle and saddle. Pulling her horse up before she got close, Shaunna watched the two.

It was a Norman Rockwell picture, all warm and fuzzy. And though she'd sworn off men, she had to admit there were times when she thought about being married, having children and watching them with their father. This was one of those times.

Not that Tyler would fit that picture, she knew, and smiled as she checked her horse to see if he was cool enough to put up. Actually, Tyler looked very awkward working with the bridle, and he was still wearing loafers and light-colored slacks. The man was not a cowboy, not by any means. Here at the barn, he stuck out like a sore thumb, all class and sophistication. He fitted in at that accounting firm he worked for, however. There, she was the one who felt like the misfit. It was just so obvious. She and Tyler were as opposite as night and day.

Which was why she couldn't understand why she found him so attractive. All night, she'd thought about his kiss. Lying in bed, she'd tossed and turned, playing it over and over in her head and wondering how far they would have gone if she hadn't stopped him.

She'd wanted him to make love with her, which had been a total surprise. Not that she didn't like men and never had those urges. She simply thought she'd gotten them under control.

"Forget him!" she muttered.

"What did you say?" one of the riders with her asked, and Shaunna suddenly remembered she was not alone. The three she'd taken on the trail ride were still in the saddle and close by. Certainly close enough to hear her.

"Nothing. Just that I, ah…" She groped for an answer. "I need to call the vet to castrate that stud colt. I can't forget him."

Two of the riders moved off, taking their horses to the arena to continue riding. Chris Prescott, Jeffery's mother, stayed. Since she often hung around to talk, Shaunna thought nothing of it. And the conversation started out perfectly normal.

"When you call the vet," Chris said, "tell him I need Mischief's teeth checked. The way he's been tossing his head when Jeffery rides him, I think there might be a problem in his mouth." Then she looked directly at Tyler and Lanie and lowered her voice. "He's certainly good-looking. I suppose he's married."

"No, he's divorced, but his ex-wife died a few months ago." Shaunna glanced Chris's way, disturbed by the feeling of jealousy that cut through her. "Why? Are you interested?"

Chris laughed. "Are you kidding? I've seen the way he looks at you. And the way you look at him. I'm not into wasting my time. Besides, if you're smart, you'll keep him for yourself."

Shaunna knew she wasn't smart. If she were, she'd tell Chris she was all wrong, would deny any interest in Tyler. Instead, she said nothing.

Shaunna was in the small barn, working with the young stud colt when she heard footsteps and looked up. It was Tyler. "We're leaving," he said. "Lanie's already in the car."

"How'd it go?" Shaunna asked, stepping out of the stall and blocking the doorway with her body so the colt couldn't escape.

"Pretty well, I think. At least we talked today. Mostly about horses, but we talked." He grinned. "She's convinced I know nothing, and she's right. She wants to come out again tomorrow, wants to bring more carrots."

"Okay with me as long as she doesn't feed them to him by hand. I don't want her losing any fingers."

"She'd also like to ride again. She says she'll behave this time."

"Then we'll give her another chance. I think it's going to be hot tomorrow. Tell her either to come early in the morning or late in the afternoon. I don't want to work the horses in the heat of the day."

He grimaced. "I have a golf game at eight-thirty and we're supposed to get together with my folks in the evening."

"If you want, drop her off early in the morning, before your game. She'll be fine."

He hesitated a moment, then nodded. "Okay, I think I'll do that."

She expected him to leave then. Instead, he stood, looking at her. She prayed he didn't mention the kiss they'd shared. She didn't want to talk about it. Talking might make it real.

Finally, he smiled. Awkwardly. "Well, I guess, ah…"

His gaze swept the length of her, and she knew he was remembering, just as she was remembering. Slowly, she shook her head.

"Until tomorrow, then," he said, and turned away.

She watched him walk out of the barn, then sighed. It had been a long time since she'd felt this way, all achy and discombobulated. She thought she'd outgrown that kind of

behavior, thought she'd learned how to ignore a physical
yearning. In the past few years, staying busy at the stable
had been enough for her. It hadn't mattered that she had
no time to date. Why bother if you weren't interested in
getting involved? She wasn't a masochist.

Shaunna heard the colt move behind her and turned
slightly to look back at him. Not fast enough, though. She
saw his open mouth just before it closed over her arm. Felt
his teeth clamping down like a vise. The pain was immediate, her cry ear shattering. The colt released his hold,
jumping back, the whites of his eyes showing. She knew
she'd scared him, but she didn't care. Grabbing her arm
just below the shoulder, Shaunna could feel the moist
warmth of blood soaking through her sleeve.

She glared at the young stud. "You—" she growled.
"Have a date with the vet."

Yet she knew it wasn't completely the colt's fault. He
was a young male, doing what many young studs did to
gain attention. It was one of the reasons they were castrated
and turned into geldings. Her error had been in thinking
about a man and not paying attention to what she was doing.

If anything, she'd been given the reality check she
clearly needed.

Chapter Six

Shaunna shook out the pills for the two horses with arthritis, the action taking more effort than usual, then carefully placed the pills in the appropriate containers where she kept each horse's medicine. The stiffness and pain in her right arm hampered her movements, and once again she chided herself for not paying more attention to the stud colt the night before. The last thing she needed was a banged-up arm and an emergency-room bill.

Or a man distracting her.

Every minute she'd spent in the emergency room—all one hundred sixty-eight of them—she'd berated herself for her recent behavior around Tyler. She'd let him talk her into taking a horse she didn't have the room or time for, had let him distract her so she broke a glass and messed up her kitchen floor, and she'd let him kiss her...messing up her mind.

She didn't have time for this.

"I brought Lanie and three pounds of carrots."

The sound of Tyler's voice—just when she'd been think-

ing of him—startled her. Without thinking, she loosened
her grip on the bottle of pills in her hand, then felt it begin
to slip. She grabbed for it, but the jab of pain that shot
down her right arm stopped her. With a groan, she watched
the plastic container hit the floor of the feed room, its con-
tents sailing everywhere.

"I'm sorry," Tyler said, standing in the doorway, looking at her. "I didn't mean to frighten you."

"Frighten" wasn't the word to describe what he did to
her, but she wasn't going to admit that. "You didn't. I just,
ah..." She decided it was better not to explain why she'd
had to let go and knelt to pick up the pills, her efforts
clumsy. "You must think I'm a real klutz." She looked at
the pill bottle. "At least I didn't break anything this time."

Tyler stepped into the feed room and got down beside
her, joining her in reaching for the pills. "The way you
were concentrating on what you were doing, I should've
realized you didn't hear me."

Shaunna chanced a glance his way and wondered what
he'd say if he knew her temporary deafness had been due
to thoughts of him. She hoped he didn't notice the bulging
bandage under her right sleeve. She didn't want to have to
explain that, either.

"Lanie was eager to get here. When I didn't see anyone
around, I decided I'd better find you, make sure you were
here and knew she was here." He dropped some of the
pills back into the bottle.

Shaunna tried to edge to the left as a protective measure
for her arm. She forgot the feed bin behind her. Her right
arm hit against it. Just slightly. Barely a tap. Still, a sharp,
quick pain cut through her, and she groaned automatically.

Frowning, Tyler looked at her. "What's the matter?"

"Oh, just a little accident I had." She forced a smile.
"Colts will be colts." The lift of Tyler's eyebrows said he

didn't understand, and Shaunna knew she'd have to explain, like it or not. "That stud cold nipped my arm yesterday."

"The one you were working with when I left?"

"Yeah." *The one I should've been paying attention to instead of you,* she thought. "It was foolish of me to turn my back on him. One of the reasons he's here is because of his biting."

"How bad is it?" Tyler's gaze moved to her right arm.

She considered telling him the injury was nothing, then decided her limited range of motion would prove that a lie. The truth was better. "I now have a dozen stitches holding me together, plus a lot of bruising. It looks terrible, but it's no big deal."

"That's all bandage?" His gaze traced the bulge of gauze and tape under her sleeve. The wrapping extended from just below her shoulder to just above her elbow. When he looked back at her, his expression showed his concern. "You shouldn't be out here working. You should take it easy, give your arm a rest."

"Sure." She laughed, the idea of taking it easy a joke. "And who's going to feed the horses and give them their medicine? Who's going to give the riding lessons I have scheduled for this morning?"

"You have a barn manager, haven't you? He can feed the horses for you. And you can cancel the riding lessons. It's Sunday. A day of rest. I'll take Lanie home. She can feed her horse carrots tomorrow or the next day."

He had it all worked out and she appreciated his concern, but he obviously didn't understand her situation. "Tyler, I can't cancel classes. That's how I make my money. And you're right, today is Sunday. I give my barn manager the day off."

"Then I'll help you." He took the pill bottle from her

hand and began gathering the rest of the spilled pills in earnest.

"You're going to help me do chores?" She scanned his outfit. As usual, he was dressed too nicely for the barn. "Wearing those clothes?"

He paused to glance down at his white golf shirt, tan slacks and brown loafers, then went back to picking up the remaining pills. "So, I get a little dirty."

"At this rate, you're going to owe a fortune in cleaning bills." She put her good hand on his. "I'm fine, Tyler. Just a little incapacitated. I've had worse things happen. I'll get everything done, just not as quickly. You go play golf."

He shook his head. "I can't play golf and leave you like this."

"Yes, you can." She liked that he cared, but she knew his suggestion was foolish. He'd be more of a hindrance than a help, and she certainly didn't want him hanging around the stable all day. Maybe it would be good for Lanie, but it wouldn't be good for her. Simply being in the same room with him made her as skittish as a colt. Standing, she held out her hand for the pill bottle. "You know nothing about horses. I'd be spending all my time trying to explain things. I can get my students to help."

He glanced in the direction of Magic's stall and paddock. "Lanie can teach me what to do."

Shaunna knew he wasn't listening. "Correct me if I'm wrong, Tyler, but I gathered that you weren't just going to that golf course this morning to set up a game. You already have one scheduled, right? Others are expecting you?"

He hesitated a moment, then shrugged. "So? Golf dates can be canceled."

"But why disappoint the others? Not that I don't appreciate your offer, but I'd better not sit around and baby this arm. If I do, it will really stiffen up. Trust me, if I really needed your help, I'd ask."

He slanted her a look. "You're sure?"

She was sure…sure he looked too good and smelled too good, his aftershave a yummy aroma that tempted her to nibble along his smooth jaw just for a taste. Until she figured out why she kept reacting so crazily around him, she wanted distance between them. "Give me those pills, say goodbye to Lanie and go," she ordered, and again held out her hand for the bottle.

He didn't hand it to her. Instead, his gaze slid to her lips, and she felt her stomach tighten. Memories of the kiss they'd shared in her kitchen came flooding back: Tyler on his knees in front of her, looping his arm around her neck and enticing her with those blue, blue eyes of his. She should have resisted then, should have said no. She should have stopped him when he drew her to her feet, stopped him when his hands began caressing her body. That she'd stopped him at all was a miracle. She credited her instinct for self-preservation to some hidden reserves of inner strength and maybe the fact that she knew Maria was in the other room and might have woken up at any moment.

Tyler Corwin was the kind of man country-and-western singers sang about. If she let him, he'd do her wrong, would break her heart. He would leave her.

After all, men she cared about always left her.

"Go," she repeated, more forcefully this time. "And when you say goodbye to Lanie, if you can convince her to help me until the others arrive, that would be wonderful."

"She'll help you," he said with conviction, then sighed and finally handed her the pill bottle. "Okay, I'll go, but I'll be back just as soon as my game is over. And then if you need any help—"

"I'll ask," she finished. "Thank you."

He stepped back, then paused, clearly reluctant to leave. "She's acting a lot better, I think. Spending the day with her yesterday seemed to help." He smiled tentatively. "I think it was something I said, but I'll be darned if I know what."

"Maybe, or maybe she just needed to know that you cared."

"Could be, I guess." He kept looking at her, and Shaunna forced herself to show no reaction. After a moment, he nodded. "I'll say goodbye to Lanie."

She watched him walk down the aisle between the stalls. On the radio, another country-and-western song was telling a tale of love gone astray, and Shaunna knew sending Tyler away didn't guarantee she wouldn't experience heartbreak. For some reason, she was attracted to him, felt a warmth around him that she hadn't felt in years. She didn't understand it, and that scared her. She didn't want to be hurt again.

Shaunna discovered that Lanie was a good helper. And Tyler was right; Lanie's attitude was much better. "Magic came closer," she said as she helped Shaunna put away the horses after the morning lessons. "Much closer than yesterday."

"He does like those carrots, doesn't he?"

"He always has. My mother said carrots were a good treat for a horse."

The way Lanie looked at her, Shaunna knew the girl was waiting for her reaction. "Carrots are good," Shaunna said cautiously. "As long as you're careful how you feed them. And they're much better than sugar."

"That's what my mommy said, too. I don't think they ever fed him, do you? I mean, at the other place. Or brushed him. He's got sh…'' She stopped herself, then glanced Shaunna's way. "He's got poop all over him,'' she finished.

Shaunna appreciated Lanie's effort not to swear but made no comment, keeping the conversation on Magic instead. "He's had it pretty rough. He didn't know what happened to you and suddenly he was in this terrible place. You're going to have to be very patient with him. He's got to learn he can trust you again.''

"People are a lot like horses, aren't they?''

The child's perception caught Shaunna by surprise. "You mean about learning whom you can trust?''

"No.'' Lanie looked down. "I mean, I know how Magic feels. It's hard for me to understand what happened…that my mommy is dead. We were driving along and all of a sudden I heard Mommy make this sound and say 'Oh, no' and then…'' Lanie raised her head, tears glistening in her eyes. "I miss her…and George.''

"Oh, Lanie.'' Shaunna wasn't sure how the child would react, but she didn't care. Using her good left arm, she drew Lanie close and hugged her to her side. "It's been rough for you, too, hasn't it?''

She half expected Lanie to pull away. Instead, the girl put her arms around Shaunna's waist, and Shaunna felt her give a deep, shuddering sigh. "I wish that man hadn't driven his car into ours. I wish my mommy and stepdaddy hadn't died.''

"Of course you do.'' Shaunna kept her arm around Lanie and continued holding her close. "But always remember that both your mommy and stepdaddy loved you very much. And even though they're gone now, you have your daddy, and I can tell he loves you, too.''

"What if…?'' Lanie drew back slightly, looking at her with eyes that were way too serious for a ten-year-old.

"What if he just *has* to take care of me? What if he's only being nice because the law is making him take care of me?"

"No, he's not being nice to you just because he *has* to be." Shaunna was sure about that. "You can tell the difference. My mother *had* to take care of me after my father deserted us. Otherwise, she couldn't get any money from the government. But she didn't want me and made sure I knew she didn't."

"How did she make sure you knew?" Lanie asked, her expression concerned.

"Well…" Shaunna remembered well. "She didn't touch me except if she absolutely had to, and she was always criticizing everything I did. She wouldn't go to any of my school events. And I never got any gifts from her. Not even at Christmastime. She said she was required to feed me, clothe me and keep a roof over my head. And, by golly, that's all she did."

"She sounds mean. Really, really mean." Lanie wrinkled her nose. "Like a wicked witch."

Shaunna smiled. "Witch" wasn't exactly what she would call her mother, but it was close enough.

"You don't still live with her, do you?" Lanie looked toward the house.

"No, I don't. I ran away when I was sixteen." As soon as she said it, Shaunna realized that wasn't the thing to tell a troubled child. Quickly, she tried to rectify her error. "But running away didn't solve my problems. It only made them worse."

"I thought about running away," Lanie admitted. "But I didn't know where to go."

"Neither did I." Shaunna smiled ruefully, remembering. "I thought I would find my father. Not that he was that great a father. You've got a much, much better one. Yours was there when you needed him. Mine didn't want to be found."

"He's only around 'cause he has to be."

"No," Shaunna said, but she wondered if the girl wasn't right. Had Tyler come back into Lanie's life only because he was required by law? If so, at least he was performing his duty well. "He really cares for you, Lanie. I can tell from things he's said. And look at all the time he spent with you here yesterday. He wouldn't have done that if he didn't care about you."

"Yeah." Lanie smiled. "He really doesn't know anything about horses, does he?"

"No, he doesn't. So you'll have to teach him."

Lanie nodded, then grinned and hugged Shaunna. "I like you."

Surprised, Shaunna hugged her back. "And I like you."

The Tuesday after the Fourth of July, Tyler was in his office, his door open, when Alicia rapped lightly on the door frame, then came in. "You busy?" she asked.

"No," he said, pushing the papers in front of him aside. As usual, Alicia looked stunning, her hair up in a sophisticated twist and her nails polished a shade of red that matched the trim on her business suit.

"Good." She closed the door behind her and walked toward his desk. Casually, she sat in one of the two leather chairs in front of his desk, crossing her legs and resting her elbows on the arms of the chair. "I think we need to talk."

Her seriousness made him uncomfortable and he chose his words carefully. "About what?"

"About us...about our future." She smiled slightly. "About setting a wedding date."

"A wedding date?" That wasn't the subject he'd thought she would bring up.

"I've been thinking a lot about this, Tyler." She uncrossed her legs and leaned slightly forward. "Actually, I made up my mind a couple of weeks ago, and I'd hoped we could discuss the matter over a candlelight dinner with soft music in the background. But lately you've been so wrapped up with your daughter and this horse of hers, I finally decided coming here would be better."

She was all business, but Alicia was always that way. She wasn't one who believed in overt displays of emotion. She'd told him that the first time they went out, and it had been fine with him. He'd learned to distrust words and gestures of love. They could always be faked.

Still, Alicia's matter-of-fact marriage proposal was taking him by surprise. He wasn't sure what to say. But it seemed he didn't need to say anything. Right away, she began her pitch.

"Tyler, you and I have been going out for almost a year now. The first time I met you, I found you interesting. You're intelligent, relatively good-looking, physically and mentally healthy, and, as it's turned out, you've shown that you can be a caring father. I'm an only child, at the peak of my childbearing years, and unmarried. My family has had money for several generations, and one of these days, I'll inherit that wealth. At least, all that the government doesn't take.

"Problem is, being an only child, and with Uncle Gordon and Aunt Emily not having any children, after me there'll be no more heirs to pass this money on to. Which means I have an obligation. I need to produce an heir or heirs for the Fischer fortune. And this isn't an obligation I take lightly. Basically, for the past two years, I've been looking for a potential mate. And, as far as I can see, you would work out fine."

Tyler stared at her. She certainly wasn't sugarcoating this. "I would work out fine?"

The way she straightened in her chair, he knew he'd upset her by questioning her. And her brusque response confirmed that. "You know what I mean."

"What I think you mean is that you want us to get married so I can father a child with you, thus producing an heir to inherit the family fortune."

"You make it sound as if it's all for my benefit. There'd be benefits on your side, too, Tyler. For one, you now do have a daughter to take care of, and you've expressed a concern over the sitters you've hired. I plan on quitting my job once I'm pregnant. I would be home for Lanie as well as the baby."

"I still feel as if we're discussing stud service."

"Don't be silly. If I'd only wanted that, I would have looked into artificial insemination. Or had a baby out of wedlock. No, I believe children should have a father and a mother, should be created the natural way."

He wondered if a marriage of convenience could be considered "natural" but didn't say anything. And he agreed with her about children needing both parents. In the past few weeks, he'd discovered the benefit of discussing problems with a woman. Shaunna was giving him new insight into Lanie's thinking.

Too bad he hadn't had more insight into Alicia's thinking. Maybe then he would have been more prepared for this conversation. Now that he thought back, a lot of his conversations with her had centered around family values—what he considered important and unimportant. At the time, he'd thought they were just idle chatter. Now he realized she'd been quizzing him, judging his responses.

"There would be, of course, a prenuptial agreement," she said. "Should we split—get a divorce—you'd have no claim to the Fischer money. But, as long as we did remain married, you would receive an annual stipend. More than enough to buy the clothes and vehicles you might want for the social events we'd be expected to attend.''

"Now it's sounding as if I'll be a kept man." And he didn't like that.

"Not kept. Certainly not. I assume you would stay on at Smith and Fischer. You'd be the logical one to oversee my trust and financial matters. With my approval, of course."

"Of course." With Alicia, he had a feeling that meant she'd check every entry. "You seem to have this all worked out."

"I've tried to think of everything." Once again, she leaned forward. "Look at it this way, Tyler. Maybe you and I aren't madly in love, but that could be to our advantage. We've both had past experiences that have made us leery of love. You with your ex-wife. Me with those former suitors who were just after my money. You've also said that you're concerned about Lanie, about leaving her with strangers so often and how you're going to deal with her when she's a teenager. What I'm offering is an arrangement that will be beneficial to both of us. I want to have a child. You need a mother for your daughter. We get along well. Have mutual interests. I think it would be an excellent merger."

"Merger," he repeated, and smiled. How like her to use that term.

"All right...arrangement." She rose gracefully to her feet and looked at her wristwatch. "I've got an appointment across town in half an hour and I don't know how long it's going to take. Why don't I call you tonight?"

"You expect my decision then?"

"No." She smiled and started for the door. "But I hope you'll have thought about it."

She left his office, and Tyler could only sit where he was, stunned.

There was a knock on his door. Before he could respond, the door opened and Gordon Fischer stepped into his office. Gordon closed the door behind him and walked toward Tyler's desk. He was smiling. "I just saw Alicia. She was in a rush as usual, but she did say you two are talking marriage."

Tyler wasn't sure how to answer that. "The subject did come up recently."

"Wonderful," Gordon said, beaming, then reached across the desk to shake Tyler's hand. "Congratulations."

Tyler didn't respond. "We haven't actually decided to get married, Gordon. To be honest, the idea took me somewhat by surprise, and I'm not sure this is the right time. There's Lanie...her horse..."

Gordon let his arm drop back to his side, a frown creasing his forehead. "And that horse woman?"

"Shaunna?" Tyler was surprised that Gordon had brought her up. He hadn't mentioned Shaunna at work, and Gordon had met her only once.

"Whatever her name is. Just the other day, Alicia said you've seemed distant since meeting her."

"It's only been a couple of weeks or so." And he hadn't been aware that he'd acted any differently around Alicia. Actually, in the past two weeks, he'd had little time for Alicia.

"The time element isn't important." Gordon continued studying him, his expression serious. "She's an attractive woman. That was obvious when I saw her here in your office. Probably would be good in bed, but she certainly wouldn't do anything for your career or your social status, if you know what I mean."

Tyler got the message. Gordon meant he had a choice.

Good sex or a rise up the career ladder and acceptance by Bakersfield's upper echelon. Alicia would ensure him both.

Choose Shaunna and…?

Suddenly realizing what he was thinking, Tyler shook his head. "Gordon, this is ridiculous. The woman is working with Lanie and Lanie's horse, that's all. I'm not sleeping with her. For heaven's sake, I have nothing in common with the woman. Absolutely nothing."

"As long as you're aware of that." Gordon looked back toward the closed door. "You and Alicia would make a good match. When she suggested I interview you for this job, I knew she was serious about you."

Gordon's comment bothered Tyler. Alicia had urged him to put in an application, but he'd thought he'd gotten the interview on his own merit. He considered himself a top-notch accountant, had graduated from college with honors and had excelled at his last job. Now he was beginning to wonder how great a part Alicia had played in his getting the job. It seemed that getting custody of Lanie hadn't been the only surprise over the past year.

"Tell you what," Gordon said, smiling. "My wife and I are having dinner with my brother and his wife a week from Friday. Why don't you and Alicia join us? We're going to the country club. It would be like getting the whole family together."

The perfect time for announcing an engagement, Tyler realized, knowing that was what Gordon was implying. He hesitated, considering his options, but Gordon didn't give him a choice.

"We'll expect you there," he said firmly, then stepped back from Tyler's desk. "Now, I'll let you get back to work."

Three hours later, Tyler knew he was between a rock and a hard place. "There's going to be a barbecue at the stable," Lanie said enthusiastically as he drove her home. "A week from Friday. Shaunna calls it her midsummer get-together. We'll go on a trail ride—Shaunna said I can use one of her horses, and you can ride in the hay wagon with the other parents who don't ride—and then there'll be a bonfire and music and everyone is going to be there."

"A week from Friday," he repeated slowly.

"Yeah. And I told Shaunna we'd bring gelatin. Everyone is bringing something, and I can make gelatin. Mommy taught me. So you won't have to do anything. Won't it be fun?"

"Honey…" He wasn't sure how to tell her. "I'm not sure I can go."

"Why not?"

He saw the light go out of Lanie's eyes and hated what he was saying. "I've, ah, I may have to go to a dinner party that night."

"But everybody's going to be there," she insisted, her eyes filling with tears. "It's going to be much, much better than any old dinner party."

"Probably so, but this is, ah, a business dinner."

"With Ah-lee-sha?" Lanie sneered the name.

"Yes. And with her parents and her uncle and aunt. Her uncle is my boss, remember?"

Lanie stared at him. "You're going to marry Alicia, aren't you?"

"I'm—"

She didn't let him finish. "You're gonna, I know you are. And when you do, you're not going to want me around."

"That's not true," he said, pulling into the garage. He turned off the engine and twisted in his seat to face her. "I'll always want you around."

"Yeah, sure. You don't even want to go to the barbecue with me." Lanie glared at him, and he waited for the verbal assault. Then he noticed her lower lip was trembling.

"Lanie?" he said softly.

"Not going to things is one way Shaunna said you can tell when a parent doesn't want you." She jerked open her door and got out of the car.

"Lanie, honey…" Tyler quickly alighted from the driver's side. "I do want you. I just can't—"

"I'm not your honey," she snapped, then went to stand in front of the door to the house, her arms crossed in front of her and her head turned so she wasn't looking at him.

He unlocked the door and pushed it open, sensing he was losing whatever ground he'd won the weekend before. "We need to talk," he said.

She looked up at him. "Are you going to marry Alicia or not?"

"I'm not sure. I'm thinking about it. It might not be a bad idea." At least, he'd been trying to convince himself of that.

Lanie shook her head and marched into the house. She headed directly for her bedroom, and Tyler followed, every step of the way trying to think of how to explain to a ten-year-old why marrying Alicia would be good for both of them.

By the time he reached her room, Lanie was sprawled across her bed, her head buried in her pillow and her stuffed animals gathered around her. He saw the picture of her mother, which usually sat on the nightstand, clutched in Lanie's right hand. And he heard her sobs. "Lanie," he said softly, not sure she would hear him.

She lifted her head and looked at him, and he wished Shaunna were around to tell him what to do next.

Chapter Seven

"This party is that important to you?" Tyler asked, the ramifications of what he was thinking playing through his head.

Lanie glared at him. "It's a barbecue."

Tyler knew what would be barbecued at Gordon Fischer's country club. *He* would be if he went to a party Shaunna was hosting instead of dining with the Fischers and making an engagement announcement. Gordon's message had been all too clear that afternoon.

"I've just gotta go," Lanie said wistfully, looking at him.

"Gotta, huh?" He smiled. It seemed that everyone had an agenda.

"You could even ask Alicia to come, if you wanted."

"I suppose I could." Though he knew what Alicia's reaction would be to that idea. She'd made her feelings clear about horses and stables. That Lanie had suggested it, however, was a breakthrough.

"So you'll come?" Lanie sat up, her expression hopeful. "To the barbecue? You'll go with me?"

"I'm thinking about it." He just wished it was a simple decision.

"It'll really be fun. Really, really fun." Lanie put her mother's picture back on the nightstand and came over to him. "Much more fun than an old business dinner."

Tyler grinned. Lanie had her mother's persistence. She was also probably right. He doubted dinner with Alicia's parents and aunt and uncle would be fun. And it bothered him that Gordon was assuming he'd be there.

Well, Gordon Fischer was wrong. If this barbecue was important to Lanie, then he was going to the barbecue, and Alicia would just have to understand. He'd made headway with Lanie; he didn't want to jeopardize that.

"Well, as long as this barbecue is going to be 'much more fun,' I guess my decision is made." He ruffled Lanie's hair. "So now shall we think about dinner?"

"Yeah." Tears gone, Lanie smiled at him, then scooted for the kitchen.

Tyler followed more slowly. When Alicia called that evening, he would explain the situation. He would even invite her to the barbecue as Lanie had suggested. And if she was still interested in discussing marriage, well, they'd discuss it.

The night of the barbecue, the weather was perfect. A slight breeze kept the insects from being too bothersome and the temperature comfortable, and after an hour of riding, most of the crowd were ready to head back to the stable and food. The sun was well on its way toward the horizon when Shaunna signaled for everyone to stop. Those on horseback let their mounts stretch their necks, while Tyler and the others in the hay wagon found relief from the bouncing.

When Tyler first climbed aboard, he'd noted that the hay wagon only had four bales of hay. The seven other adults and four young children who accompanied him around those bales didn't seem to mind the lack of padding on the wooden slats. They were too busy talking and laughing, but he couldn't seem to find a comfortable position and would have appreciated a little more cushioning. He was beginning to think he should have taken Shaunna up on her offer to rent him a horse for the ride. Then again, considering he'd only been on one a couple of times in his thirty-four years, both times at Barbara's insistence, he doubted that he'd have fared any better with a horse.

Besides, from the wagon, he could keep an eye on Lanie and Shaunna, and he'd been thoroughly enjoying that experience. Lanie was definitely happy, and Shaunna...well, Shaunna was simply a pleasure to watch.

Nearly everyone who boarded a horse at the stable had turned out for this midsummer ride and barbecue, and at least half of Shaunna's riding students had rented horses for the evening. From the time they'd left the barns, Shaunna had been busy making sure everyone was having fun.

At the moment, she was riding from one group to the next, saying something then moving on. What she said, he couldn't tell, but she was now riding toward the wagon, and he had a feeling he'd find out.

"How's it going?" she asked, her words for everyone, but her gaze meeting his.

"Wonderful. Great," he heard the others call out happily. He simply nodded in agreement. There was no sense in complaining about the bruises on his bottom.

"Good," she said. "We're going to take the horses for

a short lope, but you're going to stay here. I'm having the less experienced riders stay with you. After that, we'll cool the horses off and call it a night. It's time to gas up on some of that chili Maria made.'' Shaunna grinned. ''And I do mean gas up.''

The others laughed, and Tyler smiled. He'd seen the pot of chili by the bonfire. It was loaded with red beans.

With a nod, Shaunna spun her horse away from the wagon and cantered back to the riders. She made riding look so easy, barely moving in the saddle, but he'd seen how some of the others bounced on the back of a horse and knew looks could be deceiving.

Earthy. That was how Alicia had described Shaunna. Tyler had to agree. She was earthy and natural and damned exciting to watch, whether she was riding a horse or walking from the house to the barns. Maybe opposites did attract. He wasn't sure, but he knew they didn't have much in common and yet he found her attractive. Attractive and arousing.

He shook his head. Those were not the thoughts he should be having.

He'd told Alicia he had to attend the barbecue for Lanie's sake. That was what he had to keep in mind. He was here for Lanie…not to fantasize about Shaunna.

He'd also told Alicia he didn't want to be rushed into a decision, and she'd taken the matter quite well, he thought. Although she'd turned down his invitation to join them, she'd said she understood his need to go. She also said she was sure he'd see the logic to her plan.

On paper, marrying Alicia did look logical. Maybe it was his accounting background, but he'd made a plus and negative column, and the plus column had definitely won out. First of all, marrying Alicia would provide female companionship for Lanie. A mother figure. The negative was

Lanie wouldn't talk to Alicia right now. But he felt that would change, given time.

Alicia would provide female companionship for him, as well. She'd be an adult in the house to talk to and bounce ideas off. A hostess and a date. A partner for sex. He couldn't think of any negatives to that.

Third, marrying Alicia would help his career. Over the telephone, she'd practically promised him a vice president's title in her uncle's firm.

Tyler wasn't sure if that was a positive or a negative. Although he liked the idea of becoming vice president, he was a man who needed to earn a position on his own. And he wasn't sure being a vice president at Smith and Fischer was what he wanted. In the back of his mind, he'd always envisioned owning his own accounting business. If he married Alicia, that dream would be out of the question. He knew she wouldn't leave her uncle's firm.

Finally, if he married Alicia, he'd be emotionally safe. It wouldn't be a marriage based on love, but he didn't want love. Being in love put you in danger of being hurt. Made you vulnerable. He'd been there. Done that. Now he wanted an arrangement that would be satisfying and safe.

Nevertheless, he'd chosen to come to the barbecue with Lanie, while Alicia had gone to the country club with her parents and her aunt and uncle. And he was glad that was how it had worked out.

He could just imagine how Alicia would have reacted if she'd come along tonight. From the moment they stepped out of the car, she would have been complaining. She wouldn't have liked the dirt and dust, or the smell of the horses, or the discomfort of riding in a wagon. She certainly wouldn't have been impressed with the pot of chili hanging by the bonfire or the rack of ribs on the grill. Alicia didn't eat chili or ribs. For that matter, he doubted Alicia would have been very impressed by the others attending the barbecue.

He, on the other hand, was thoroughly enjoying himself. Well, except for the bumps and bruises. Some of the group on the ride he'd met before. There was Chris and her son, Jeffery. Chris had tried to talk him into riding a horse and even offered one of hers, but he'd declined her invitation. He'd also met Bobby, whose parents couldn't make it. The boy wasn't the monster Lanie said he was, but Tyler did note that Bobby teased Lanie a lot.

Probably the couple he found the most in common with were the parents of a girl Lanie liked and spent time with at the stable. Patti Shaw was two months older than Lanie; her mother, Rita, was a teacher, and her father, Chuck, a dentist. They also had a son, Tommy, who was only four. The three of them were riding in the wagon with Tyler, while Patti was riding with Lanie. Watching Lanie with Patti, the two girls giggling at everything, made him think Lanie's doctor had definitely been right. Horses, Lanie's passion, had been the catalyst to bringing her back to normal.

He'd already seen a change in her physical appearance. Working at the barn was making her stronger and giving her more color. And her attitude had improved greatly in the past few weeks. The anger wasn't as evident. At least, not as often. Nor the resentment.

His heart went out to the little girl. There was so much she didn't understand, so much he wished he could tell her. Problem was, he couldn't tell her, not without making matters worse.

It was after eight when Shaunna stood back from the bonfire and watched the others. All that remained of the barbecued ribs and chili that Maria had prepared was a pile of bones and a stack of empty, dirty bowls. The salads and desserts the others had brought had filled out the selection of foods, and if anyone went away hungry, it was their own fault. Even the dogs and cats were too full to move.

Todd, her stable manager, had brought his guitar and begun playing after the food was eaten. Judy, the teenager who boarded her Appaloosa at the stable and had a crush on him, had settled herself at his feet and was singing along with the others who'd joined in. The evening was going exactly as Shaunna had hoped.

She liked it when she could get all of her boarders and students together. There were no better people, to her way of thinking, than a group of horse lovers. It didn't matter what they did for a living or how much or how little money they possessed; they shared a common love and that was enough to bind them together. And the fact that they had come to her, followed her teachings, was proof to her that these people truly did love their horses.

Her gaze drifted to Tyler.

He was probably the only non-horse person in the group, yet she saw hope for him. The fact that he'd brought Magic to her and hadn't wanted him destroyed was proof that he had a horseman's heart, whether he knew it or not. And the way he treated Lanie proved he had a father's heart, as well.

She wanted to condemn him for deserting his child for so long, yet she couldn't. Why he hadn't bothered to see Lanie during that time was a mystery to her, but Shaunna knew he wouldn't leave his daughter now. Seeing him sitting on the ground next to Lanie, his denims so new they practically crackled when he moved, Shaunna had to smile. At least he'd worn something appropriate. He was learning.

He glanced her way, and Shaunna felt an instantaneous giddiness. She hoped it was the chili. She didn't like the sensations that curled through her every time Tyler looked her way. It brought back memories of the time when she was twenty-two and as infatuated with Dale, one of Betsy Helman's boarders, as Judy was with Todd now. Shaunna remembered all too well how foolish she'd been and how much it had hurt when Dale left. She didn't want to feel that way again. She didn't want to make herself vulnerable.

She looked down at the ground and kicked a pebble with the toe of her boot. Damn the sexual attraction. She wasn't going to let it get to her. She might not be the smartest person alive, but she was no fool.

Except she'd foolishly let Tyler kiss her that one night. And she foolishly kept thinking about him, dreaming about him. She had to stop it…if she only knew how.

She heard footsteps coming toward her and looked up. Tyler had left Lanie's side and was heading in her direction. As he neared, she fought down an impulse to run. She wouldn't let him know he made her nervous. So what if her legs suddenly felt shaky? Leaning against the fence, she could hold herself up. And he certainly couldn't tell that her pulse was racing.

At least, she hoped he couldn't.

"Nice party," he said, easing himself into position next to her. "I think this is the most fun I've had in a long time."

"Lanie seems to be enjoying herself." Shaunna wanted to steer the conversation away from them. Talking about Lanie would be safer.

"I'm glad I let her talk me into coming."

"She said you were supposed to be somewhere else. A business meeting or something?"

"Or something."

She could feel the energy of his presence. It was racing through her, putting her on edge, and she kept her eyes on Lanie. "I think we're going to be able to start working with

Magic next week. He's adapting nicely, comes to her when she calls now and takes the carrots from her hand. And she's been watching me work with the other horses. I think she understands what I'm doing."

"She says you talk to the horses."

Shaunna shook her head and chanced a quick glance his way. "I don't talk to them. I listen to them. I watch what they're telling me."

He smiled that wonderful, sensuous smile of his. "And what do they tell you?"

"They tell me…" She looked away again, knowing what she'd read in his look. The attraction she felt was not one-sided. "They tell me," she tried again, "if they're unhappy or scared." Right now, she was scared. Scared of the feelings Tyler aroused. "They tell me if they're ready to listen to me or not."

"So you do talk to them."

"Well, I guess you could say I do." She laughed nervously. "Basically, I tell them I'm not going to be a threat, that they can trust me."

"And can they?"

"Yes. I won't hurt them. I get them to do what I want by letting them think it's what they want to do. If they think running from me will be good, I let them run. And when they decide they want to stop running, I let them stop. I give them choices."

"Life seems to be made up of choices."

He sighed, and she glanced his way. He was staring at his daughter, who was talking to Patti. Shaunna had noticed a friendship building between the two girls. "They seem to be getting along quite well."

For a moment, he looked at her as if he didn't understand, then looked back at Lanie. "Yes, you're right. And she needs friends her age. Needs female companionship."

"I think we're about to be besieged by the two of them." Shaunna watched Patti and Lanie head toward them. The way the girls were grinning and nudging each other, Shaunna was sure something was up.

"Patti wants me to spend the night at her house," Lanie said to Tyler. "Can I, please?"

"Tonight?" He hesitated.

"Please?" Lanie pleaded. "It's all right with her parents. They said she could ask me. You can ask them." She pointed toward Patti's parents and Shaunna saw Tyler glance in their direction. Patti's parents both gave a nod, and he turned to Lanie.

"What about your clothes? You don't have a nightgown with you...or a toothbrush."

"She can borrow one of my nightgowns, Mr. Corwin," Patti said. "And my father's a dentist. We always have extra toothbrushes."

"Please?" Lanie begged again.

Tyler appeared to be giving her plea some thought, then he smiled and ruffled Lanie's hair. "Sure, why not?" He glanced at Shaunna. "I think I'd better find out where they live. See you later."

He walked away, the two girls bouncing around his feet, and Shaunna watched. The easy way he'd accepted Lanie's request had touched her. He was trying so hard to be a good father. The guy was just plain lovable.

Not that she would fall in love with him, of course.

The stars were out and the fire had burned down to embers by the time everyone headed for home. Maria had gone to bed. Only Shaunna sat on one of the benches by the fire pit, watching the coals and remembering the songs that had been sung and the jokes that had been told. Evenings like this made her feel as though she belonged to a family.

Maybe just a family of horse lovers, but a family nonetheless.

Car headlights caught her attention. She watched the vehicle pull into the parking area, the yard light distorting its color. It wasn't until the driver stepped out and the dogs went racing up to greet him that she recognized Tyler. He started for her house, but she called to him. "I'm over here."

Hearing her voice, he walked toward her. "I left my jacket," he said. "Decided I'd better come back for it."

"Oh." She held up a jacket one of her guests had brought her. "This it?"

"That's it."

"Should have known." She chuckled. "It looks brand-new."

"It is. What are you doing?" He strolled over to the bench where she sat and took the denim jacket she handed him. But he didn't seem in any hurry to leave.

"I'm just enjoying the night." She poked at the dying fire with a stick. "Did you have a good time tonight?"

"I had a great time." He eased himself down next to her. "So did Lanie. Do you do this often?"

"I try to do it a couple times a year. Once midsummer and again in the fall." She smiled, remembering. "It was something Betsy used to do. For her, the people who boarded at the stable were family, and I guess for me it's…"

She let her voice trail off. No sense in going on about why she did it. She was feeling maudlin, and he wouldn't be interested in her need for a family. Wouldn't understand.

"You guess for you it's…?" he asked, and picked up a stick to poke at the coals with her.

"A tradition." That said it well enough.

"Started by Betsy." He glanced Shaunna's way. "She was the woman who originally owned this stable?"

"Yes. Most of what I know about horses I learned from her."

"In that case, she must have been a remarkable woman."

"She was."

For a few moments, they sat in silence, each pushing coals around with their sticks, shaking out the flames when the ends caught on fire. Shaunna was aware of every movement Tyler made, every breath he took.

She knew that was foolish, that she had to get her mind off him, had to stop letting him affect her. She groped for something to talk about. "What kind of business meeting did you miss tonight?"

He chuckled, which she found strange. She saw he was gazing at her. He smiled. "It was supposed to be a dinner to announce my engagement to Alicia Fischer. But I couldn't make it, not after what you'd said to Lanie."

"What did I say to Lanie?" She certainly couldn't think of anything she'd said that would have stopped him from announcing his engagement. She hadn't even realized he was engaged. If she had, maybe hearing him say it wouldn't have just felt like a punch in the stomach.

"You told her if a parent didn't go to functions with his child, it meant he didn't love her."

"I didn't say that," Shaunna started to explain, then remembered. "What I said was that my mother never went to any of my school functions. Never did anything with me. We were talking about how to tell if a parent loved you or not. I didn't think she'd take it that literally. I'm sorry if I messed up your engagement party."

He shrugged. "It wasn't a party, just a family dinner."

"I gather, then, that your friendship with Alicia goes deeper than you thought?" She knew she shouldn't let it bother her. She should be happy for him. "Let me offer my congratulations."

"Yeah, well…" He tossed his stick into the coals and looked at her. "We're not actually engaged. It's something I'm thinking about."

"Thinking about?"

"Alicia and I are discussing the possibility." He paused before abruptly asking, "Have you ever been in love, Shaunna?"

His question took her by surprise, and for a moment she wasn't sure what to say. Then she decided to be truthful. "I once thought I was. Turned out it was a delusion. I was in love with the idea of being in love. And as it turned out, he didn't love me. I just thought he did."

"Same here." Again, the fire held his attention. "With Lanie's mother."

He didn't go on, and the silence crept up on her. An uneasy silence of things left unsaid. Finally, she couldn't stand it any longer. "And?"

"That's all. As you said, love is a delusion. Relationships need a more stable basis." She had a feeling she understood what he was saying…or not saying. "Are you telling me that you're not in love with Alicia?"

"Let's say I'm looking at marriage in a much more logical fashion. Marrying Alicia would definitely have benefits. I need to consider Lanie's welfare."

"And you believe marrying Alicia will be in Lanie's best interest."

"That's what I'm trying to decide."

She knew she should stay out of Tyler's business, but from what Lanie had said, she didn't see a marriage between Tyler and Alicia as a good decision. "You and Lanie seem to be getting along much better."

"Better, yes, but sometimes I'm not quite sure what to

say to her. When she was a baby, all I needed to do was make a few faces and we were communicating. Now…" He reached down and picked up a piece of bark by his feet and tossed it into the coals. It flamed almost instantly. "Lanie said your father left you when you were little."

"Not so little. I was almost nine when he took off."

"You haven't seen him since?"

"No. He used to tell me that if an Indian didn't want to be found, he wouldn't be. I guess he was right. I went looking for him when I was a teenager, but I never found him. Then, again, he was only part Indian, so I may still run into him someday."

"And if you did, what would you say to him?"

"I'd ask him why. Why he left me. Why I could never do anything to please him."

"And if he told you he'd left because he thought that would be the best thing for you, what would you say?"

"I'd tell him he was wrong. Is that why you left Lanie, Tyler? Why you never contacted her?"

Tyler nodded.

The pain she saw on his face touched her heart. She placed a hand on his arm. "At least you're there for her now. Just don't leave her again."

He placed his own hand on hers, giving her fingers a gentle squeeze. "If I were your father," he said softly. "I'd tell you I'd been a fool to leave you, that you're perfect."

Shaunna knew, if she were perfect, she wouldn't be thinking the thoughts racing through her head.

Chapter Eight

Looking into Tyler's eyes, Shaunna was sure she'd lost her mind. Here she'd spent the evening telling herself she wasn't interested in him. He'd just told her he was engaged. Yet the touch of his hand had her heart bouncing around like a rodeo bronco. She needed to git while the gittin' was good. "I think I'd better go in," she said, and started to rise to her feet. "It's getting late."

"Stay." He tightened his grip on her hand, stopping her. "Please?"

The squeeze of his fingers sent butterflies dancing in her stomach. No man had excited her like this since her escapade with Dale. She'd been an idiot back then, and around Tyler she wasn't acting much better. A look from Tyler could frazzle her thoughts. A smile and she turned clumsy. Every time he came to the stable, she was on edge and ready to make a fool of herself.

Except this time she wouldn't.

"Tyler, you just told me you're getting married. You shouldn't even be here." She worked her hand free from his and moved farther down the bench. Maybe she wouldn't leave, but she needed space. Lots of space.

He stared at her, then frowned. "What's my getting married have to do with my coming back to get my jacket?"

"You know what I mean."

She thought for a moment he would deny the sexual tension between them. Or worse, tell her that she was imagining it. Then he took in a deep breath and stared at the dying embers. "You're right. The jacket could have waited until morning. I came here hoping you'd still be up. It was all quiet at home without Lanie there, and I started thinking about how much fun it had been tonight and how great you'd looked, and the next thing I knew, I was in my car driving back here."

She didn't say anything, but in her heart, she felt a small thrill that he'd come back to see her and that he'd thought she looked great. Not that it made any difference under the circumstances. "Although I'm flattered, if you were lonely, why didn't you go see your fiancée-to-be?"

"Go see Alicia?" He chuckled wryly. "Alicia doesn't see anyone after nine-thirty at night. Or before she puts on her makeup in the morning. She's rather set in her ways."

"So you came here."

"Yes...I came here. But if I'm keeping you up...or bothering you, I'll leave. I guess—" he shrugged and looked away "—I guess I just wanted to talk."

He was bothering her all right, but Shaunna wasn't about to admit that. And since she was up and he just wanted to talk and she supposedly wasn't interested in him—couldn't be—she shouldn't care if he came by, should she? "Talk to your heart's content."

"Thanks." His smile showed relief. "I guess I didn't want the night to end. I really did have fun. It reminded me of my college days, back when Barbara and I were dating. We used to go to all the football bonfires. Sing songs. Not country-and-western songs, but the atmosphere was the same as tonight. Sort of like one big happy family.''

Shaunna marveled at how closely his feelings mirrored her own. ''They're a good group. So you and your ex went to college together?''

''Met there our last year. Eloped right after we graduated. That first summer, we were like two peas in a pod, then I got a job, and Barbara got a job, and we had less time together. Still, for almost three years, I thought everything was fine, especially when Lanie was born. Then I discovered it was all a delusion.''

''And you walked away.'' Shaunna poked at the coals. ''With my dad, he left a note, said he'd had it, and that was the last we heard of him.''

''I didn't exactly walk away. Barbara told me quite clearly that she didn't want to hear from me. She had other plans. After that…well, I went a little crazy. It took me a while before I finally came to my senses. I decided to join the navy, serve my country. Since getting out, I've been concentrating on my career.''

''And now you have your daughter living with you and you're getting married again. Sounds like you're back with the living.''

''Yeah.''

He graced her with a crooked smile, and she felt the all too familiar butterflies take flight again. Immediately, she reminded herself that he wasn't available and that she wouldn't have wanted him even if he were. ''It's too bad Alicia couldn't have joined you and Lanie tonight.''

His smile disappeared. ''We did invite her. I knew she'd refuse. Horses and barbecues are not Alicia's things. The country club and elegant restaurants are more to her taste.

Silk and marble, not denim and pine. You saw her that afternoon in my office. She's accustomed to mingling with presidents and CEOs of major companies. Her family owns land and oil wells, and Alicia is the only daughter. Bouncing around in a hay wagon would not have entertained her.''

''Wow, sounds like you'd be marrying into money.''

''Lots of money, that's for sure. More than I'll ever earn. And I'll admit, I'm not opposed to the idea. I'm a lot like Alicia. I like nice things. I truly was surprised I had as much fun tonight as I did. Tomorrow, however, I'll probably be cursing the bruises I got from that wagon.''

''I think Lanie really appreciated your coming tonight.'' Shaunna glanced around the stable area, her gaze stopping on her house. ''If your Alicia had come, it sounds like she'd have been appalled by this place. It isn't exactly the in spot for the jet set.''

''It grows on you,'' he said, his voice so soft that Shaunna turned to look at him. He was staring at her, his smile too warm and tender for her comfort.

Quickly, she averted her eyes. ''You do realize Lanie's not that wild about your Alicia, don't you?''

''I know. But up until recently, Lanie wasn't wild about anyone, so I'm hoping her attitude will change in time. And to be honest, up until last week, I hadn't thought about getting married to anyone. I've had my hands full these past few months trying to get things straightened out with Lanie. Alicia is the one who suggested the idea. And it does sound logical. I don't know what to do with a daughter. I had brothers, not sisters. With Lanie, half the time I'm groping in the dark about what to say or how to react. All I can think is that if it's bad now, what's it going to be like when she hits her teens?''

''I do hope you realize being a woman doesn't suddenly

make you all-knowing…or even a good mother. I had one who proved that. And, in my opinion, you're doing a great job with Lanie. It's simply going to take her awhile to adjust to you and accept that her mother's gone.''

"I know." He nodded in agreement. "And you've been a big help, Shaunna. I want you to know that."

Shaunna said nothing, and Tyler looked her way. In the darkness, he could barely make out her features. Only her sigh gave any indication of her feelings.

"Do be careful, Tyler," she said. "I like your daughter. I'd hate to see her hurt."

"And so would I." He touched her again. Just a hand on her arm. He needed the contact, needed her to understand. "You've helped. Helped a lot. The past few weeks have been a real breakthrough with Lanie. She's talking to me now, and I feel I owe that to you."

"I haven't done anything special."

She didn't need to. *She* was special. He couldn't explain how. He simply felt it. "Horses talk to you, and people talk to you."

"Only if they want to."

And he wanted to. Crazy thing was, he wanted to tell her more, wanted her to know how she confused him and ask her why his thoughts turned crazy every time he was near her. He'd wanted to kiss her earlier—wanted to kiss her now—and that was definitely not a good reaction for a man who was thinking of getting married. Not a good feeling for a man who didn't want to feel.

"I'd better go," he said, quickly standing. "It's late. Too late for you to be listening to me going on and on."

"I didn't mind." But she also stood, keeping a distance between them.

He stooped and grabbed his jacket off the bench, then

straightened so he was facing her again. "I'll see you around. Okay?"

She said nothing until he was walking away. Then she called after him, "Tyler, whatever you do, don't make a mistake."

"I won't," he called back, but he knew he already had. He never should have come back tonight.

"You've got to come." That was what Lanie had said to him that morning. "Shaunna's going to saddle and ride Magic this afternoon, and maybe, if he acts all right, I'll be able to ride him. She said if you wanted to watch, you should come around three."

He glanced at the clock on the dash of his car. It was five minutes to three. He was right on time.

He pulled into the stable yard and parked. He was beginning to recognize the vehicles that were there on a regular basis. The battered blue truck was Shaunna's. The red compact was Maria's— who, he'd discovered, lived at the house and had for thirty of her forty-nine years.

The green van was Chris Prescott's, and a gray four door belonged to Bobby Hunt's mother. The infamous Bobby, who was Lanie's sworn enemy.

Every night, Tyler heard stories about that "yucky, stupid Bobby" who was always at the stable and made fun of her and called her horse ugly. Tyler might have thought there was a serious problem if he hadn't noticed at the barbecue that Lanie did just as much teasing.

When Tyler found Lanie, she was standing outside the round pen. Bobby was there, too. As soon as Lanie saw Tyler, she turned to Bobby. "See, I told ya he'd come."

"So? Big deal. Your horse still sucks."

"Does not."

Tyler realized nothing had changed. But he was glad

he'd taken time off work despite Gordon's parting comment about his needing to get his priorities in order. Watching Bobby make a face at Lanie, Tyler knew he did have his priorities in order. It was important for him to be here this afternoon.

Lanie positioned herself next to Tyler though she continued making faces at Bobby. Tyler watched the two for a moment, then looked around. Magic was already in the round pen, but Shaunna was nowhere to be seen. "She's getting everything ready," Lanie said, answering Tyler's unasked question.

"Good." He took a moment to watch the horse. "He looks good."

Magic had changed dramatically in the five weeks since he'd been brought to Shaunna's. A full ration of grain and alfalfa pellets was covering his ribs with flesh, and repeated brushings by Lanie, once Magic let her touch him, had removed the caked manure and brought the luster back to his coat. Though not in perfect condition, he looked much healthier and fitter. He also looked suspicious as he watched the group outside the pen.

"Ready?"

Hearing Shaunna's voice, Tyler turned toward her. She carried a Western saddle and bridle and had a whip and saddle pad squeezed under her armpit. As usual, the instant he saw her his heart skipped a beat and his pulse started racing. He was getting used to this reaction. Not that he liked it.

Everything, except for the whip, was dropped outside the gate to the round pen. He nodded when Shaunna looked at him, and she nodded back. He'd avoided talking to her since the night of the barbecue. It seemed safer to simply pick Lanie up and drive off. Shaunna made him think foolish things, and even now, his first thought when he saw her was that Alicia had been right. Shaunna looked earthy. And desirable, especially the way her jeans hugged her hips and the material of her sleeveless T-shirt had been pulled taut across her breasts when she was carrying the saddle.

The bandage was long gone from her arm, only the line of a scar showing the bite she'd gotten from the colt—a gelded colt now, from what he'd heard. Lanie had explained everything. He wasn't sure he liked her knowing all that.

Shaunna watched Magic as she spoke to Lanie. "He knows something's up. See how he keeps shuffling his feet and flicking his ears. I think we'll play on that fear for a while until he acknowledges that he wants to talk. While I'm working with him in there, I'll explain what I'm doing and what you should look for. After I've ridden him for a while, if I feel he's safe, I'll put you up on him."

"He was safe before," Lanie said. "I could do anything I wanted with him."

"And you've brought him a long way in the past five weeks. He's remembering what you and your mother taught him." Again, she looked at Tyler. "I'm glad you came."

"I wouldn't have missed this," he said, wondering if the heat he felt in his face was a blush. Now that would be something. He never blushed.

Shaunna opened the gate and stepped into the pen, then closed the gate behind her, the rawhide whip in her right hand. Magic was watching it, prancing nervously and warily moving back away from her.

"We know he's afraid of the whip," Shaunna said, loud enough for everyone to hear, especially Lanie. "We know he was whipped at that other stable. And you told me, Lanie, that the man your mother hired to break Magic used a whip." She kept hers low and by her side so it dragged behind her. "What I want is to see if my having a whip riles him, and for him to learn that the whip itself is nothing to fear, that I'm not going to hurt him. Otherwise, someday, somewhere, while you're riding him, he'll see a whip—or something that looks like a whip—and he'll freak out.''

She stopped when she reached the middle of the round pen and faced the horse. He was watching her…and the whip. She moved the whip higher so he could see it, and his ears bent back. He snorted and paced, and she flicked the whip so it made a cracking sound. Magic's eyes went wild, but rather than lunging at her, he spooked, dashing away from her as he circled the pen.

Shaunna kept herself positioned so she was always facing him, the whip clearly visible. Magic frantically galloped on and on as she calmly spoke to those outside the pen. ''That's good. He ran rather than attacking. Now we just play on his instincts. Horses are basically lazy, and after a while, he's going to get tired and realize he hasn't been hurt, so he's going to slow down. But I'm not going to let him stop, not right away. What I'm doing now is the first step in teaching a horse forward impulsion, so we might as well get a lesson in. And I also want him to reason this all out and decide for himself that the whip isn't going to hurt him and carrying on is a waste of his energy.''

Tyler noticed the horse slow, then saw Shaunna snap the whip, making a noise but never touching the horse. Magic broke into another wild dash. She did that several times, forcing the horse to reverse his direction twice in the process. Tyler began to understand the beauty of a round pen. The horse could run all he wanted, but he was always the same distance from her.

''He's getting tired now,'' Shaunna said. ''Wants to talk this over. Watch for him to flick his inside ear toward me and for the look in his eyes to soften. There. He's telling me he's tired of all this running, and since I haven't hurt

him, if there's anything I have to say, he'll listen. Next
he'll lower his head, bring it closer to the ground."

Tyler watched the horse shift to a trot, the ear flicking
toward Shaunna, then his head dropping lower so the
horse's nose was only inches from the ground. The wild,
glazed look was gone from Magic's eyes, and he was
watching her.

"When he starts making chewing motions with his
mouth, licking his lips," Shaunna said, "he'll be ready.
He'll have come to an understanding." Magic's tongue
came out, and Shaunna smiled. "Good. Now, I'm going to
stop being a threat." She turned away from the horse, not
even looking at him, and Magic stopped dead still, his eyes
fixed on her.

Shaunna walked away from him, and Tyler held his
breath. Five weeks earlier, he'd seen Magic try to attack
Lanie. It seemed incredible to him that Shaunna would now
turn her back on the Mustang. But she wasn't even watching him.

Magic hesitated, then began following her just like a
puppy dog. Shaunna grinned at Lanie. "He's saying, 'Wait,
don't leave me.' Since I pose no threat, his instinct as a
herd animal tells him to stay with me."

When Shaunna stopped, so did Magic. When she took a
few more steps, he followed, each time coming closer. Finally, when Shaunna stopped once more, Magic came right
up to her and nudged her on the shoulder. She turned to
face him. He didn't run off, and she touched him, rubbing
first his neck, then his shoulders and back.

When Shaunna ran the whip over the horse's body, using
it to scratch him, Magic only sniffed at it. Tyler was
amazed. The saddle pad came next. Then the saddle.
Slowly, she introduced each to Magic, allowing him to
sniff, then rubbing him with the item, and finally putting it

on his back. Just as easily, he accepted the bridle and snaffle bit. When the horse was completely saddled and bridled, Shaunna ran him around the pen again, repeating the routine from earlier. But it only took two circles before Magic bent his ear her way, lowered his head and began to chew at the bit. Tyler glanced at his watch when Shaunna settled herself in the saddle without Magic even flicking his tail. The entire process had taken half an hour. The wild horse that had been starved and whipped and turned into an animal that no other stable owners wanted to handle now stood calmly waiting for Shaunna to tell him what to do.

Tyler knew he'd witnessed magic.

Shaunna walked the horse around the ring once, then nudged him into a slow trot. Though she held the reins, she put no pressure on the bit. Which direction the horse went wasn't important. Right now, all she wanted to do was reestablish trust, let him reason that having her on his back was no big deal.

The way he was responding pleased Shaunna, and she could see no reason why Lanie couldn't get on him. After all the time Lanie had spent cajoling the horse close enough to touch, then brushing his coat, she deserved a reward. And Shaunna was sure Lanie wouldn't do anything foolish. She'd proven herself a decent rider and was no longer rebelling against every order Shaunna gave. The girl would listen to instructions.

Nudging Magic with her leg, she guided the Mustang over to the gate. "Want to ride him?" she asked Lanie.

"Yes." The girl's eyes brightened, and she scooted over to the gate, almost all signs of her limp gone.

Shaunna started to swing off Magic's back. It was then that Jeffery Prescott made his presence known. The six-year-old came running around the end of the barn, chasing Bobby Hunt's mother's Jack Russell terrier, all the while swinging a lariat over his head and making loud, hooting sounds.

The muscles in Magic's back tightened, and Shaunna knew what was about to happen even before it did. She'd shown Magic that the whip posed no threat, but Jeffery's chasing that dog, hooting and swinging that lariat, most definitely looked like danger to the Mustang.

She tried to swing back into the saddle, but it was too late. Magic swerved away from the gate and the boy, giving a stiff-legged hop as he did. If she'd been in the saddle, she could have easily turned with him. As it was, she was caught off balance. Like a sack of grain, she was tossed to the side.

For Tyler, everything happened too fast. He'd heard the boy, but by the time he'd looked in that direction, out of the corner of his eye, he also caught sight of Magic, the wild look of fear again in the horse's eyes. The horse spun around and bucked, and Shaunna went flying.

He saw her head hit the fence post, actually heard the sound. His stomach knotted with fear. A simple fall to the ground was one thing. Falling might break a bone or cause bruises. A head injury was something else. A blow to the head could be disastrous. Fatal. It had been fatal for Lanie's mother, and the head injury Lanie suffered in the accident had almost killed her.

For a moment, he could only stare at Shaunna's inert form on the ground. Then the adrenaline kicked in, and he ran, swearing when the gate didn't immediately open. Once through, he dashed to Shaunna's side. Kneeling beside her, he touched her arm, afraid of what he might find.

"Shaunna?" She gasped for breath, and he knew she was alive. Then she turned her head slightly to look at him, and a faint smile said she recognized him. The relief that swept through him was tempered with concern. He knew

enough first aid to know her neck and back had to be sta-
bilized. "Don't move. Lie still."

"I'm…I'm okay." She ignored his order and did move.
Rolling to her side, she pushed herself halfway up to a
sitting position.

He tried to stop her. "You need to lie down. You might
have broken something."

She slowly rotated her head, rubbing her hand along the
back of her neck, then touched her left temple. "I think I
hit my head."

"You did. On the fence post." He glanced at the one
nearby, then looked at the spot on her head that she was
touching. A lump was beginning to form. "You may have
a concussion."

Again, she gingerly rotated her head. Then she looked
across the pen. He followed her gaze and saw Lanie with
Magic. The girl was stroking the horse's neck, talking to
him. And close behind her was Bobby. "Is he all right?"
Shaunna called to Lanie, wincing the moment she spoke.

Lanie nodded at her. "Just scared. You okay?"

"Shaken up a little, but I'll live. Keep telling him everything is all right." Shaunna grabbed Tyler's arm. "Help
me up."

"No. You need to stay down." He didn't know how to
make it any clearer, but he might as well have been talking
to the fence post. She was already struggling to her feet.

So he helped her, steadying her by slipping an arm
around her waist when he felt her begin to sway. She
looked at him, her eyes dazed. "We need to get the horse
untacked and back to his stall."

"Can Lanie do it? Where's your stable manager?" He
glanced around for Todd.

"Send Bobby for him and make sure Jeffery's not swinging that lariat anymore. Magic wasn't ready for that."

Again, she rubbed her neck and head. "*I* wasn't ready for that."

She called to Lanie, grimacing as she did, "Bring him over here." The girl complied, and Shaunna also spoke to the horse, touching him and fussing over him. Then she nodded to Lanie. "Lead him back to his stall. We'll untack him there. I don't think you'd better ride him today."

Tyler could tell that Lanie was disappointed, but she just nodded and gave a slight tug on Magic's reins. "Come on, boy. Time to go."

Shaunna started toward the barn, then stopped. She looked at him, and Tyler knew something was wrong. The color vanished from her cheeks and her eyes took on a vacant look. And then he realized she was sinking in front of him. Reaching out, he grabbed for her before she hit the ground.

Chapter Nine

At seven-thirty that night, Shaunna was sitting up in her bed, pillows stuffed behind her back and an ice pack freezing the left side of her head. She'd just spent three and a half hours in the emergency room, had a pounding headache and a sick feeling that she was going to go bankrupt simply from doctor bills. But she couldn't complain, not with Lanie and Maria standing at the end of her bed looking so worried, and Tyler sitting next to her, holding her hand as if she might vanish if he let go.

"I'm fine," she told them, afraid they would hover there all night if she didn't say so. "I saw a few stars for a moment or two and heard a few rockets go off, but I'm okay now. How's Magic?"

Lanie answered. "He's fine. He was really sorry he threw you off. He didn't mean to. He just got scared when he saw that rope."

"I'm not blaming him." Shaunna knew Lanie needed the reassurance. "Or Jeffery." Though she'd have to talk to Chris. The boy could cause a serious accident if he wasn't watched more closely.

"Bobby scared the cra—the poop out of Jeffery," Lanie said, giggling. "He won't be swinging any ropes around Magic again."

Shaunna wondered what Bobby had done to Jeffery. She'd probably better talk to Bobby's mother, too.

Turning her head slowly and carefully, she looked at Tyler. "I suppose I should thank you for taking me to the hospital and staying with me."

"You mean, in spite of all your protests?" He grinned.

"I knew it wasn't anything serious." Still, it had been good to hear that from a doctor, and she had appreciated Tyler's being with her. If not for his badgering the staff, she'd probably still be sitting in the emergency room waiting for a doctor to see her. Then again, if not for him, she probably wouldn't have gone to the hospital in the first place and she wouldn't have another emergency-room bill looming on the horizon.

"You had us all so worried," Maria said, her accent more pronounced than usual, which always happened when she got upset. "You sure you're okay?"

"I'm fine," Shaunna repeated. "I have a headache, that's all."

"She has a concussion," Tyler corrected. "And has to be checked every four hours during the night. Just like it says on that sheet I gave you. You're sure you don't mind doing that?"

"Is no problem." She frowned at Shaunna. "But you stay in bed like doctor said."

"What about my chores?" Though Todd managed the big barn, the small barn was her responsibility, and she always checked the horses before turning in.

Maria slipped a plump arm around Lanie's shoulders,

drawing the girl close, just as she'd done when Shaunna first came to the stable twelve years before. "Lanie and I, we help Todd feed and give the medication. All done. I do final check later. Now we go to fix dinner. Right?"

Maria looked down at the girl, and Lanie nodded and grinned back up at her. "Right." Then Lanie looked at Tyler. "We can stay and eat here, can't we?"

"Sounds good to me." He squeezed Shaunna's hand. "I don't often get a home-cooked meal that I don't have to prepare myself."

"So you stay in bed," Maria said to Shaunna. "Rest." She nodded toward Tyler. "Talk to him while Lanie and me, we take care of everything."

Watching Maria and Lanie leave the room, Shaunna felt that matters had been taken out of her hands. But she wasn't sure she wanted to talk to Tyler, and it wasn't just the headache. She was upset with him.

She'd told him she didn't need to go to the hospital. Maybe he had good medical insurance, but she didn't, and she certainly didn't like dealing with all those bills doctors and hospitals liked to send. Even someone without her problem would get confused. Heck, she hadn't even paid the bill for her last visit. And that was for a real emergency, not just a bump on the head.

Sure, she'd gotten light-headed in the yard and sort of blacked out. But that was no big deal. She'd regained consciousness soon enough. She didn't need a doctor telling her she was going to have a goose egg and to take two aspirins and call in the morning if she felt worse.

"Well, I should let you get some rest," Tyler said, but he didn't release her hand and he didn't give any indication that he was leaving.

Shaunna saw the concern in his expression and she knew

she couldn't stay angry with him. "I'm fine," she said for the umpteenth time.

"You do have a concussion."

"A *slight* concussion. That's what the doctor said. Slight."

"You passed out."

"I must have moved too quickly. That's all." And made a fool of herself—again—though it had been rather touching, coming to in his arms as he carried her to the house. Not many men could have carried her the way he had. For an accountant, Tyler Corwin was in pretty good shape.

She smiled. The man was in damned good shape. And he was damned good-looking and damned considerate. If he didn't stop looking at her that way, she was going to start telling him how wonderful he was, how great it had felt with his arms wrapped around her, and how she'd loved it when he'd started yelling at everyone in the hospital, making them get help for her. Oh, yeah, she could really make a fool of herself.

"What's so funny?" he asked, cocking his head to the side.

"I do seem to be accident-prone around you."

"I hope you've got good insurance."

Her smile disappeared. "I wish."

"You don't?"

"Oh, on the stable, I carry the best liability insurance that's available. I have to. And I have excellent coverage for anyone hurt on the premises. But to cut costs, I took a higher deductible on my coverage."

"How high a deductible?"

"Oh, I don't know. The exact numbers escape me." As they always did. "A couple thousand dollars, I think. Something like that."

He sat back in his chair, still holding on to her hand.

"So basically you only have insurance for major medical and these emergency-room bills will all have to come out of your pocket?"

"I'll manage." She had to.

"It was Magic who put you in the emergency room this time. I'll take care of the bill."

"No, you won't." She frowned and pulled her hand free from his. "A trainer knows getting on a problem horse is chancy. Heck, riders take chances every time they get on a horse. I knew Magic wasn't spookproof. I should've been better prepared, ready for something like Jeffery coming at us with that rope. I can't let you pay. It's part of the business I'm in."

"I'm paying." He grinned. "And you can't stop me. I'll just wait until the bill joins the others on your kitchen table, then I'll sneak it out and you'll never know it's gone."

"Not funny."

"Have you ever considered getting out of this business?" He glanced at her right arm where the colt's bite had left a scar and at the ice pack on her head. "You don't seem to be making any money here and you're putting your life at risk."

"Stop working with horses? And do what, Tyler? Work at a fast-food restaurant? In an office? Impossible for me."

"Not impossible. People change careers all the time. I heard somewhere that the average worker will have eighteen jobs in a lifetime."

"Fine, but I'm not your average worker. I'm no good with numbers. What's easy for you isn't for me. And I'm not walking away from this place. Never. It was entrusted to me, and I'm going to take care of it."

Tyler saw tears in her eyes, and that surprised him. He'd seen her in pain and not once had she shed a tear. Now, just because he'd told her to find another career, she was crying.

"I'm sorry. I shouldn't have said anything. I'm sure you feel an obligation here."

"No, it's not an obligation, Tyler. It's a gift. You just don't understand. I was sixteen years old when I came here. I'd run away from home, had hitchhiked and walked from Arizona to California. I was living out of garbage cans and sleeping wherever I could find a spot when I stumbled onto this place. Except, I don't think I did stumble. I think some divine guidance led me here. Who knows how I might have turned out if not for Betsy."

"That's the woman who owned this place before you?" He thought that was the name.

Shaunna nodded. "I think she knew I was a stray from the moment I stepped onto this property. Oh, I pretended I was interested in taking riding lessons, and she gave me a tour of the place, but I don't think I fooled her. I came back after dark. I figured I'd steal whatever cash was in the box I saw one of her students put money into, then be on my way before anyone found out. But it sure didn't happen that way."

"She caught you stealing?"

"'Found' is a better word. I didn't figure into my plans a sick horse that Betsy was checking on during the night. She caught me taking the money, told me to keep it if I needed it, then went and invited me in for something to eat. Before I'd finished, she'd offered me a job and a place to stay. And I stayed. She didn't ask questions, simply waited until I was ready to tell her what had happened."

Shaunna stared down at the chenille spread she was sitting on. "This was her room back then. Her bed. She treated me like her daughter. Gave me everything I'd never had. Love and acceptance."

"What about your mother? Wasn't she looking for you?"

"Shoot, no." Shaunna laughed grimly. "My mother didn't care that I'd run away. When Betsy did find out how old I was and what I'd done, she called my mother and talked to her. My mother was more than happy to give her permission for me to stay here...just as long as nothing was said and she could continue claiming me as a dependent until I was eighteen."

"So this became your home and you've lived here ever since?"

Shaunna nodded slowly. "And when Betsy died three years ago, the stable and land became mine."

"She willed it to you?"

"Yes. Everything to do with the horses, including the few cattle we raise, became mine." Shaunna nodded toward the kitchen. "The house is in a trust. I'm the trustee, but as long as Maria is alive, she has a home here. And Betsy also gave Maria the car, some stocks and money. That's in addition to what she'd already put aside for Maria's daughter's education."

"Boy, the woman did treat you like family."

"Because we were her family. Maria, like me, was a stray. Betsy found her when Maria was nineteen, pregnant and in this country illegally. So Betsy took her in, gave her a home, helped her get her citizenship and helped her raise her daughter. You haven't met Anna. She's really a neat gal. She's in college now and doing great."

"How old was this Betsy when she died?"

"Seventy-three. She was sixty-four when I met her. She never married, never had a family of her own. The one brother she had died when he was twenty. There were no other relatives. But she said she was luckier than most people. The way things worked out, she got to pick her family.

And that was her way. She was always going around picking up strays—dogs, cats, horses and people. Anyone with a problem. The defective ones.''

"A tradition you're following, I gather?" He was beginning to understand.

"Yes, I guess so." Again, she looked at him. "Tyler, you're probably right about this career not being the safest around, and no, I'm not going to make a fortune here, especially if I keep taking in horses others have given up on. But I can't let them go to the meatpackers, and working with horses is something I can do. I'm good with them and love working with them. So if it seems strange to you that I enjoy this, let me tell you, the idea of being an accountant and enjoying working with numbers sounds strange to me. Actually, it sounds terrifying.''

"Yeah, but numbers don't bite. Don't buck you off.''

"But Magic didn't buck me off." She gave an embarrassed smile. "He turned and I fell off.''

"Oh, Shaunna." He touched the side of her face with the tips of his fingers. "If only…''

He saw her lick her lips and remembered that she'd said when Magic licked his lips, he was signaling his willingness to communicate. Tyler knew what he wanted to communicate. He could only hope he understood what Shaunna was signalling. Shifting position, he moved off the chair and onto the edge of the bed. The mattress gave under his weight, and he leaned closer.

"You scared me today, lady," he said softly, knowing she scared him all the time. "I thought something terrible had happened to you.''

"Tyler?" She said his name hesitantly, and he knew what she was asking. He didn't answer because he didn't know the answer. He just knew he wanted to kiss her, right or wrong.

Gently, his lips touched hers. She didn't move. Not her mouth, not her body. She didn't even seem to be breathing, and he drew back slightly and looked at her.

She was watching him, her topaz eyes wide and clear. Her lips parted slightly, and he thought she was going to speak, then she smiled and reached forward, looping a hand behind his neck and drawing him close again.

This time, when his mouth touched hers, he was the one who saw stars. Heard rockets go off. Knew his world had turned upside down. He heard himself sigh. Or maybe it was her. He felt her tongue play against his lips. Moist and probing, his tongue met the challenge. Parry was met by thrust. Curiosity with knowledge.

She wasn't shy or hesitant. She combed her fingers through his hair, holding him to her, then ran her hands up and down his arms, rubbing her fingers over his skin. Her nails were short and blunt, and as they teased his skin, messages were sent to all parts of his body. He'd opened Pandora's box, and now the emotions were running rampant. Lust mingled with something akin to love. Not that it could be love, he told himself. That emotion wasn't allowed. Couldn't be admitted.

Careful around the bump on her head, he brushed his thumb over her cheek. A lingering tear had left a trail of moisture. He wiped it away, then let his hand slide down to her shoulder. Then he noticed the abrasions on her arm where soft skin had collided with hard ground and lost. He'd been so afraid when Magic threw her off. For a minute, she'd lain there so still. Deathly still. Now she felt alive and warm, and he wanted to hold her close and kiss her forever, to dip into her warmth and feel her vitality.

The urges surging through him were barely containable. He was halfway relieved when she pushed against his chest, breaking the contact between them. He sat back, waiting

for a word or signal. He was sure she could tell he wanted
to make love with her. Not that he would attempt it. Not
today. He'd just brought her back from the emergency
room. Lanie and Maria were in the other room. He could
control these crazy thoughts. He had to.

She closed her eyes, and he watched the rapid rise and
fall of her breathing. "This is probably not what the doctor
ordered," he said, his voice husky with emotion.

"Probably not," she repeated, and opened her eyes
again, a worried look replacing the languid smile that had
been on her lips only moments before. "Probably not
something we should be doing at all."

"Probably not." But he knew he wanted to kiss her
again, wanted to go on kissing her for a lifetime.

She took in a deep breath. "What about Alicia?"

Shaunna might as well have slapped him with her ice
pack. He'd forgotten about Alicia, had forgotten about Barbara and what she'd done to him.

His gaze moving to the wall behind Shaunna's bed, Tyler
tried to regain control. She had posters hanging there. Not
in frames, but tacked right to the plaster, some advertising
horse shows that had taken place long ago, others showing
panoramic scenes of Indians and horses. They were pictures
of her world, haphazardly placed and illustrating how different their lives were.

What about Alicia? he repeated to himself.

Alicia was like him. With Alicia, he was in control. He
understood her, and she understood him. They both had
goals. Ambitions. They didn't let their emotions carry them
away.

Shaunna, on the other hand, took chances, cared more
about people and horses than making money. She got emotionally involved. Openly expressed her feelings.

Well, emotions were dangerous. Emotions made you vulnerable. If you cared, you could be hurt. He didn't want to care.

His silence seemed to speak volumes to Shaunna.

"I see." She let her hands drop away from his arms. "Could you get me a glass of water, please? I'm very thirsty."

He doubted she did see, but he couldn't explain, and he needed distance. Needed time to think. He stood, the impression of his body remaining on the bedcovers next to her. He shouldn't have kissed her, shouldn't have given in to his impulses. It was best he leave. "I'll get you that glass of water and see how dinner's coming along," he said and walked out of the room.

Although Alicia had presented her proposition for marriage early in July, they hadn't discussed it any further. First there was the barbecue. He'd been the one who'd asked for time to think until that passed. Then Alicia ran into a problem with a conference. She'd had no time to talk, much less meet with him, and Tyler had put the idea of marriage out of his mind. His relationship with Lanie was his main concern.

Now, however, he knew he had to make a decision. He couldn't be kissing Shaunna and thinking of making love with her while contemplating marriage to another woman. Maybe Shaunna wasn't right for him, but letting Alicia dangle wasn't right, either.

Tyler tried calling Alicia the next morning. Her voice mail message said she was out, so he asked her to call him when she had time, that they needed to talk.

She hadn't called back by the time Gordon Fischer popped into Tyler's office and asked him to join him for lunch at the Mexican restaurant down the block. "I want your input regarding that accounting system we're thinking of buying," Gordon said.

Tyler was flattered that he was being included in the decision. "I'd be glad to join you." He stood and grabbed his jacket.

The restaurant was only a short walk, and the heat, rather than computer software, dominated their conversation. To Tyler's surprise, Alicia was waiting in the restaurant when they arrived. She already had a table.

"I tried calling you this morning," he said.

She smiled. "I didn't get your message, but I wanted to see you, too. I guess great minds think alike. Sit down." She pointed at the chair next to her. "Uncle Gordon." She nodded her greeting to him.

The moment the waiter finished getting their drink orders, Gordon spoke. "So, Alicia have you decided on a wedding date?"

"Wedding date?" Tyler gulped and knew this was going to be awkward. He'd hoped to talk to Alicia alone, explain his feelings and concerns. He turned to her.

She smiled warmly and reached over to cover his hand with hers. "We've both been so busy, honey, I didn't want to push, but we really do need to set a date."

"Alicia, I tried calling you—"

"From what my wife tells me," Gordon interrupted, "it takes months to plan a wedding. At least, a decent wedding." He regarded Alicia. "Your aunt says she'll help in any way she can."

"That's wonderful, Uncle Gordon." Alicia lifted her hand from Tyler's and pulled out a notebook from her purse. "I've been making some notes, ideas about a theme."

"Alicia, we really do need to talk first," Tyler said, hoping to stop her.

His effort was futile. She forged ahead as if everything had been decided. It didn't matter that he hadn't said he would marry her. Alicia had her color scheme decided, music, even the number of guests. Always the efficient organizer, she had a list. Finally, she paused and looked at him. "I think May would be the perfect month. Don't you, Tyler?"

"Alicia, that call this morning," he began, determined not to be interrupted again. "It was to tell you that I've decided against getting married."

"What do you mean, 'Decided against getting married?'" Gordon asked, his voice rising.

Tyler met his boss's disapproving glare. "I mean, I think your niece is a wonderful woman—" he glanced Alicia's way "—you are, you know. And any man would be proud to be your husband. But I don't feel marriage is the right thing for Lanie right now...or for me."

"You're saying you're not going to marry me?" Alicia looked stunned.

"I wanted to tell you privately." Certainly not in a restaurant in front of her uncle. "But—"

"Perhaps you'd better understand the ramifications of that decision," Gordon said, all signs of congeniality gone from his face. "Alicia feels, as her husband, you would be the perfect person to manage her finances. However, if you do not feel that marriage to my niece is in your best interest, then we certainly wouldn't want to entrust the management of her finances to you. And if I have to hire someone else to manage those finances..." He paused, a forced smile touching his lips. "Well, we can only maintain so many accountants in this firm. Someone would have to go."

Tyler knew what Gordon meant. "So you're saying if I don't marry Alicia I'm fired?"

"Fired?" Gordon shook his head. "No. But I think you

can understand the economics of this matter." Still smiling, he reached over to pat Tyler's arm. "Why don't you take the afternoon off, son? Think about this. You're a good man." He glanced at Alicia. "My niece likes you."

Tyler's first impulse was to tell Gordon to forget the job, that he quit. But Tyler stopped himself. A year ago he could have done that; being jobless wouldn't have bothered him. He was a good accountant. A damned good one. He could get another job. He could start his own firm.

Problem was, he now had Lanie to think about. No job would mean no medical insurance, and with Lanie about to start riding Magic, he needed that. He'd seen how often Shaunna was getting hurt. No job would mean cutting back on expenses, and he had Magic's board bill and training to consider.

No job would mean uprooting Lanie and himself...just when they'd started to feel like a family. A family that somehow had come to include Shaunna Lightfeather.

No, he couldn't afford to say anything rash. "I will think about it, Gordon," he said and stood. He nodded toward Alicia. "I'll talk to you later."

Chapter Ten

Tyler didn't go directly to his car. For an hour, he walked around downtown Bakersfield, staring into windows without seeing a thing. Gordon had told him to think things over, and Tyler was. He thought about his past and his future. For nearly a year he'd worked for Smith and Fischer. He'd worked hard, had built a good client base and had felt he was an asset to the firm. It appeared his major asset was his supposed ability to produce an heir.

Gordon had put it on the line. Marry Alicia, and he had a job. Say no, and he was on the street. It wouldn't happen immediately, but Tyler understood the terms.

If it weren't for Lanie, he would have given Gordon his answer in an instant. For that matter, he wouldn't have even considered Alicia's proposition in the first place. But he did have Lanie to think about.

When Tyler got in his car, he had no destination in mind. For a few miles, he simply drove. He didn't recognize the direction he was taking until he realized he was on the road to Shaunna's stable. Almost automatically, he headed there.

It was close to two o'clock when Tyler pulled into the stable yard. He knew Lanie wouldn't be ready to come home. He'd discovered that she could spend hours at the stable and still not be ready to leave. He'd just stop by, he decided. It would give him a chance to see how Shaunna was feeling.

Before he even turned off the engine, two of the stable's dogs were at the car door. They wagged their tails when he stepped out, their tongues lolling out the sides of their mouths as they panted in the heat. For the first time since leaving the restaurant, Tyler became aware of the temperature. He tossed his jacket onto the back seat, along with his tie, rolled up his sleeves and undid the top buttons of his shirt. Then he gave each dog a pat on the head and started for the house. He figured Shaunna would be taking it easy after her ordeal the day before.

"Tyler! Over here!"

The sound of Shaunna's voice came from the riding arenas. Surprised, he turned in that direction and saw her standing outside the larger arena. She was leaning against the railing, her hair pulled back in a single braid and a cowboy hat covering her head, shielding her face from the sun. Smiling, she waved him over.

He hadn't expected to see her up, much less out of the house, and he was disturbed by the tightening in his groin. He would never understand how she could look so enticing in a T-shirt, jeans and cowboy boots. Her clothes revealed little, yet that didn't stop his imagination from running rampant.

"Lanie's here." Shaunna pointed toward the arena.

He saw Lanie then. She was riding Magic, keeping the horse between the two other horses ridden by Patti and Bobby. All three horses were jogging, the slow trot barely eating up any ground. When Lanie reached the far corner, she saw him and waved. "I'm riding him," she called out.

"So I see," he called back, then quickly walked over to join Shaunna at the railing. "Is it safe for her to ride him?" He remembered how the horse had bucked the day before.

"I worked him in the round pen for a while, then rode him for a half hour. He behaved so well, I couldn't see any reason for her not to ride him." Shaunna smiled. "And Jeffery isn't around."

"You rode him?" He stared at her. "The doctor said you should take it easy for a day or two." Tyler crouched slightly so he could see her forehead under her hat. Though not as pronounced as the night before, the slight lump on her forehead had turned the surrounding skin an ugly purple.

Shaunna frowned at him and turned back toward the arena. "Yes, I have a bump on my head. I also still have work to do."

"Including riding Magic?" Maybe she needed to do some chores, but as far as he was concerned, she could have put off working with the Mustang for a few days.

"Watch your daughter, Tyler. This is a big step for her. And she's doing great. See how gentle she's being with Magic, how patient. Notice how she's talking to him, keeping him calm."

Shaunna was ignoring his concern, and Tyler knew there was no use arguing with her about what she should or should not be doing with a concussion. She'd closed the subject. So he followed her suggestion and watched Lanie, noticing how she talked to the horse and patted him often. She was also smiling as he'd never seen her smile before.

"I can't believe that's the same horse brought here less than two months ago." Or the same little girl, he could have added.

"He's come a long way." Shaunna glanced in Tyler's direction. "Today, Lanie asked me if I thought she'd be able to show him this summer. I don't know how you feel about it, but if Magic continues to come along as well as he has been, I think she might be able to."

"Show? You mean, like in a horse show?" Tyler hadn't thought about Lanie showing Magic. Getting Magic so the horse could be ridden was the only goal he'd considered.

"There's a show not too far from here in two weeks. Bobby and Patti are going. I wouldn't expect Lanie to win anything, but it would be a good experience for her."

"I suppose it would be all right," Tyler said, then remembered the reason he wasn't at work. In two weeks, he might be out of a job. "Are we talking a lot of money here?"

"No. This is just a small show. Mostly amateurs. Entry fees are low and can be paid that day." She chuckled. "Bobby's not going to be happy that I suggested this. He's been bragging about how much better his horse is than hers, and I don't think a judge will agree."

Tyler watched Bobby and his horse for a while, then Lanie and Magic. In his opinion, Lanie and the Mustang did look better. When Bobby made a face at Lanie, Tyler grinned. "I see they're still at it."

"All the time." Shaunna laughed softly. "I think it's true love, Dad."

"Oh, don't even suggest that." He certainly didn't want to think about it. "She's just a child."

"Who's growing up faster than you think. Next thing you know, you'll be walking her down the aisle."

He hated to admit that Shaunna was probably right. He'd heard parents talk about how quickly their children grew up. One day they were babies, the next they were adults. Tyler had been shocked when he first saw Lanie after the accident. She'd grown so much in the nine years that had passed. He didn't want to think of what was ahead in the next nine years: her teens, boyfriends...heartaches.

That, Tyler realized, was what he dreaded most. He hated to imagine Lanie ever having her heart broken. The way he once had.

The soft touch of Shaunna's hand on his caught him by surprise and brought his attention down to their hands, then back to her face. Amusement sparkled in her eyes. "Come on, Dad. Don't look so glum. It won't be that bad."

He hoped not. "I was thinking of all the problems she'll have to face in the next few years. The hurts."

"Hurt is part of life. They say it makes one stronger. Not that I know who 'they' are." She continued grinning, switching her focus back to the children and moving her hand away from his. "It would be nice if we could protect them, wouldn't it? Soon enough, they'll be out in the cold, cruel world." Her attention turned back to him. "By the way, what are you doing here so early in the afternoon? Get a day off or something?"

"As a matter of fact, I do have the afternoon off. To think things over."

"To think things over?" Shaunna echoed pointedly. "So what are you thinking about?"

"My future."

"Now that's a profound subject. And have you made any decisions about your future?"

"Not so far." He decided he'd better explain. "I was invited to lunch by my boss today. He said he wanted to discuss a new software program being purchased by the firm. Turned out Alicia was also at the restaurant and the meeting was about us, about our wedding."

"Ah, I see."

Shaunna glanced away, and Tyler saw a tightening of

her mouth before she looked back. He knew she didn't understand. How could she? He still didn't understand.

"I'd thought," he said, "that Alicia and I were just in the 'thinking about it' stage, but it seems Alicia has already begun making wedding plans. When I said I didn't think marriage was in Lanie's best interest right now, I received an ultimatum. Either marry Alicia next spring or lose my job."

"They can't do that, can they?"

"Alicia's uncle is my boss. He's in charge of the firm. If his niece isn't happy..." Tyler shrugged. "You get the picture."

"But he can't... He wouldn't..." Her gaze met Tyler's. "What are you going to do?"

"That's what I have to decide." And looking into Shaunna's topaz eyes, he knew he couldn't make that decision around her. She confused him. Around her, he acted without reason.

No, this decision had to be made with a clear head.

He glanced back at Lanie. "She'll be okay, won't she? I mean, I thought I'd just stop by before I take off for a while...." He didn't know what else to say.

"She'll be okay," Shaunna said softly and again touched his arm. "What about you?"

He knew he wasn't okay, not the way her touch had his heart racing. He had a problem—a major problem. Backing up, he shook his head. "I'm okay. I'm fine."

"Tyler?" Her voice held concern.

He kept shaking his head. "No, really, I'm all right. I just need to think. I'll be back at five to pick up Lanie."

Tyler turned and headed for his car, and Shaunna watched him, wishing she'd known the right words to say. The right words to soothe.

It shouldn't matter to her, she told herself. After all, it

wasn't as if she had a relationship with him. So he'd kissed her a couple of times. Two kisses didn't mean anything. He boarded his daughter's horse at her stable. That was all. They were practically strangers, certainly not lovers.

Lovers. The word sent a chill through her body.

She wasn't in love with Tyler, was she?

Shaunna made her way back to the arena, the idea too frightening to contemplate. She couldn't be in love with him. His life was completely the opposite of hers. Hormones. That's all it was. Crazy hormones. Well, she could ignore the hormones. She had to.

"Where's he going?" Shaunna heard, then noticed that Lanie had broken away from the others and was riding toward her.

"I'm not sure," Shaunna answered. "He said he'd be back at five to pick you up."

Lanie watched her father get into his car. "What did he think of me riding Magic?"

"He was impressed."

Lanie grinned and gave the Mustang a pat. "He's doing super, don't you think? It's almost like nothing ever happened, like before the accident."

Shaunna also reached over the railing to pat the horse. Magic was behaving well, but Shaunna had a lump on her head and a sore body to remember that the Mustang still had a way to go. "He's doing super, all right, but we still have to get him over his fears, and that's going to take time."

"I know. But do you think I can ride him in that show Bobby and Patti are going to be in?"

Shaunna knew Lanie wanted to be a part of the group. And the way Magic was behaving today, she didn't see any reason why Lanie couldn't show him. "Let's just see how he is in two weeks."

"Did you ask him?" Lanie nodded toward Tyler's departing car. "About me showing Magic?"

"I mentioned it to him."

"And?" Lanie's expression was hopeful.

"I think he'll let you, as long as he feels it's safe. We really didn't discuss it in detail. He has something else on his mind today."

"Probably Ah-lee-sha." Lanie made a face. "She wants him to marry her, you know."

"That's what he said. How would you feel if he does?"

"I'd run away. I'd come here and live with you and Maria."

Shaunna knew she had to be careful in what she said next. "I'm flattered that you'd want to come here, but I don't think that would be the best thing for you to do. Your father loves you and needs you. He'd be very hurt and sad if you left."

"I know he says he loves me, but..." Lanie stopped and clenched her lips together, and Shaunna saw tears in her eyes. Shaking her head, Lanie turned Magic away from the fence and jogged back toward Bobby and Patti.

"Lanie?" Shaunna called after her, but Lanie didn't look back, and Shaunna knew the child was still hurting from the years her father had stayed away. Tyler said he'd had a good reason, but how did one explain that to a ten-year-old? For that matter, how could she convince Lanie that her father's marrying Alicia was a good idea? Especially since Shaunna couldn't even convince herself.

Tyler drove down one road after another, passing houses and farms without seeing anything. In the span of a few hours, he'd walked away from two women, one who was prodding him to get married and the other who was prodding his emotions.

When his marriage to Barbara ended, he'd sworn he would never let himself get emotionally involved with another woman and would never again get married. Now he was caught between a marriage proposal and the one emotion he'd thought he could control.

Love.

It wasn't that he considered love a weakness. He did love Lanie. More than she would probably ever realize. And the way she'd been acting lately, he was sure she loved him. One of these days, she might even call him Dad or Daddy.

He smiled at the thought, remembering how Lanie had said Da Da when she was only six months old. He'd gotten so excited, but Barbara had explained it was just a natural sound that babies made and didn't mean she was calling him daddy. That was right at the time when his world had come crashing down on him and he'd discovered how phony love could be.

It was the love between a man and a woman he wanted to avoid. He certainly didn't want to be in love with Shaunna.

That kind of love was an illusion. A delusion. Barbara had proved that to him. She hadn't loved him, not after that first year or so, but he hadn't known that and thought things had been going along fine. He might never have known Barbara had a lover if Lanie hadn't had a hernia.

Maybe what he needed to do was marry Alicia. That would be a marriage with no delusions, no love. He'd keep his job. Alicia would be a mother to Lanie. Everything would be perfect.

So if everything would be perfect, why are you driving all over the countryside, Corwin? he asked himself. *Why didn't you jump at the chance to get engaged to Alicia when she first suggested it?*

He knew the answer.

She was tall and lanky and had dark brown hair and topaz eyes. She played on his protective instincts and she excited his emotions. From the first time he'd seen her, he'd been in trouble. Without his even realizing what was happening, Shaunna Lightfeather had eased her way into his heart, confusing him and wiping out any ability to think logically.

"Damn." He shook his head, wanting to deny the truth. But love was something you couldn't control.

Shaunna felt a tingly sensation skitter over her skin as she watched the three youngsters in the arena. Not sure why, she turned and looked behind her. Standing halfway between the parking area and the barns was Tyler. Her gaze met his, the tightening in her stomach immediate.

She knew it wasn't five o'clock. Barely a half hour had passed since Tyler had driven off. Did his early return mean he'd made up his mind? If so, what had he decided?

Shaunna couldn't tell from his expression. He simply kept staring at her, absorbing her with those rich blue eyes of his. And then he started walking toward her.

She held her breath, waiting for him to speak. Every step he took created more quivering in her stomach. The tension was driving her crazy.

Only when he stopped directly in front of her did he smile. Just the slightest of grins. "I made a decision," he said softly.

"And?" She steeled herself for his answer. "What did you decide?"

"That some things can't be controlled." The action in the arena caught his attention. "Lanie's still riding?"

He was stalling, clearly unable to share his momentous decision with her yet. She took a deep breath, hoping to steady her erratic heartbeat, and resolved to give him space.

She wouldn't ask him his choice. Not again. She would only expose her vulnerability at how much his decision meant to her.

She glanced at the three children in the arena. "I think we're going to have to pry Lanie off Magic's back."

"She's changed since I brought her here." His gaze Shaunna's way was warm. "Remember how she was that first day?"

"I remember."

"She was pale and weak, and most of all, she was angry. With me and with life." He looked back at his daughter. "Now she's almost as tan as you are. She's riding her horse and laughing."

"Time can do a lot. It heals the body and it heals the heart."

"So can some people. You've been good for her." For a moment, he was silent. Then he went on, "I really didn't have a decision to make. I think, deep down, I knew the answer all along. Alicia wouldn't be a good mother for Lanie."

"You're sure about this?"

He chuckled. "I'm sure that if I married Alicia, she wouldn't let Lanie go hungry or without the right clothing or anything like that. But she wouldn't give her the love she needs. She wouldn't care for Lanie as if she were her own."

"What about your job?"

"Well, I guess I'm looking for a new job." He breathed deeply, then smiled. "Actually, that might not be such a bad thing. I've learned a lot working at Smith and Fischer, and I've given them their money's worth, but I think I'd rather work for a smaller firm...maybe start my own accounting business."

"It doesn't seem quite fair."

"Life isn't always fair." He touched the side of her face, brushing back a strand of hair that had pulled loose from her braid. "You once said you were looking for an accountant. It appears that I will soon be free to accept new clients. Interested?"

Shaunna held her breath, her skin tingling where his fingers had touched. *Interested?* That was the problem. She was too damned interested.

Still, she heard herself answer, "Yes."

Chapter Eleven

Three days later, Shaunna paced her kitchen, eyeing the pile of bills on her kitchen table. Tyler was going to have a fit when he saw her books. Actually, that was the problem. She kept no records.

Every week, after she'd deposited the money that came in from lessons and board, she paid a few bills and hoped the checks wouldn't bounce. She had no idea how the stable was doing. She and numbers just didn't get along. She did need an accountant. It was that simple.

Except, it wasn't simple.

Now she was going to have to admit to Tyler that she couldn't add or subtract, much less multiply, divide or do anything more complex. Reason told her she shouldn't be embarrassed, that it was simply a handicap, just like being blind or being deaf. Well, when someone was blind or deaf, others could tell. In her case, few people knew. She'd learned to compensate, and she did it well.

But her last accountant had caught on. It was difficult enough making ends meet in the horse business without having someone you employed skimming the profits. Thank goodness Maria had figured out what the guy was doing before he walked off with all of their money.

A car pulling into the yard caught Shaunna's attention. She glanced at the clock and her stomach did a flip. It was exactly two o'clock. Tyler was right on time.

She watched him get out of his car, stretch and look around. Going to the screen door, she called, "In here."

He smiled and sauntered toward the house, looking relaxed and casual with his jacket and tie off and his sleeves rolled up to his elbows. Looking sexy as all get-out, she decided, wishing she didn't get a giddy sensation of anticipation every time she saw him.

"Is Lanie with Bobby and Patti as usual?" he asked as he neared.

"The three of them are out trail riding." Shaunna stepped back so Tyler could enter, then followed him into her kitchen. "You want some lemonade?"

"Sure."

She went to the refrigerator and took out the pitcher of lemonade that Maria had prepared. From the cupboard, she got two glasses. "Plastic," she said, holding them up for him to see. "Just in case I go knocking things off the table again."

"Plastic's safer," he said, then grinned, his gaze slipping to her mouth. "But sometimes risk has its benefits."

For a moment, Shaunna thought she might drop the two glasses she held. She understood what he meant. The benefit was the kiss they'd shared.

Quickly, she turned toward the counter, afraid he might see the flush in her cheeks. For the past three days, she'd lectured herself about her reaction around him. She would not accept that she might be in love with him. It simply couldn't be. His daughter boarded her horse at the stable and she'd hired him as an accountant, that was all. Their relationship would be strictly business.

"So, did you get everything out of your office this morning?" she asked, trying to sound casual.

"It's all cleaned out and ready for the next guy. Turned in my keys and said my goodbyes."

Shaunna brought the two glasses of lemonade to the table. "I still can't believe they fired you."

"Downsized," he said, taking the drink she offered. "If Gordon fired me, I might have had just cause for a lawsuit. But as he so properly phrased it, they regretfully had to lay me off due to downsizing."

"The guy could've at least given you two weeks' notice." Tyler was still standing, but Shaunna had to sit. She wasn't sure her legs would hold her up. Her nervousness wasn't something she'd expected.

"He would have given me two weeks." Tyler also sat. "But why drag it out? I finished the files I was working on and turned everything else over to the others. So..." He leaned back in his chair and grinned. "I'm all yours now."

"All mine?" Shaunna stared at him, her stomach doing another flip.

He nodded, his glance momentarily dropping to the pile of bills on her table. "You now have an accountant. Except—" he paused and took a sip of lemonade "—instead of hiring me, why don't we work out a trade? This job shouldn't take up all of my time, and there's no sense in your paying me, then me turning around and paying you back. Why don't I do your books in exchange for the time you put in with Lanie and Magic?"

"You want to trade your services as an accountant for lessons?" Shaunna laughed. "Wait until you see what you have to do. This won't be easy, Tyler. My last accountant was doctoring the books. You're not only going to have to figure out where we're at now, you're going to have that mess to clean up.''

''We'll work it out. You're lucky you caught him.''

''I didn't.'' And she never would have, either. ''It was Maria who started getting suspicious when the figures he gave her one week didn't match what she knew we should have made that week. So she started checking the money box before he came and discovered he was skimming off a little every day. When she confronted him with the evidence, he denied it, of course. But after I fired him, the discrepancies stopped.''

''I hope you reported him to the authorities.''

Shaunna shook her head. ''I couldn't actually prove anything, but I know he won't be giving me as a reference.''

Tyler looked at the stack of bills by his glass of lemonade. ''How far behind are you?''

''With some not far. With others, way overdue.''

''I didn't realize it was that bad. I should have offered my services sooner.''

''You were busy.'' And she'd tried to ignore the problem.

''Are these all the bills you owe on?''

''I think so. If there are any others, Maria would have them.''

''You are looking for me?'' Maria waddled into the kitchen. ''How you are doing, Tyler?''

''I'm doing fine, Maria,'' he said. ''Do you know of any other bills that haven't been paid, other than these?''

Maria looked at the stack on the table, then back at him. ''No, that is all of them.''

''Well, then, I guess this is what I start with.'' He took a gulp of his lemonade, then drew the bills closer. ''I'll also need your checking account and savings account statenents. Bank books. Credit card statements. Anything that hows how much you have or how much you owe."

Shaunna stared at him. "You're going to start now?"

"Why not?"

Why not? Because she'd figured they would meet that afternoon to work out a schedule, talk about pay and what he would need. Then once she knew his schedule, she could arrange to stay out of his way. She didn't want him to know why she wasn't doing any of the bookkeeping.

He didn't wait for her answer but picked up the top bill. "Well, I see this one was due two months ago." He glanced up at her. "Oh, and I'll also need some paper and pencils."

"I thought he was going to use the office in the barn." Maria looked at Shaunna. "Everything he needs is in there. And more quiet for you two away from my kitchen."

"He will," Shaunna assured her. "However, right now it's a mess. I was going to clean it up this afternoon."

"So?" Maria shrugged. "You two work together and clean it out. ¿Sí?"

No was more in line with Shaunna's feelings. The office in the barn was just a small room even when it was clean. Too cozy, in her opinion, to be working next to Tyler. For her emotional safety, she needed to keep a distance between them.

"Look at him." Shaunna motioned toward Tyler's white shirt. "He's not dressed for barn cleaning."

Tyler glanced down at his shirt, then back at Shaunna. "So I'll have another laundry bill. Maria's right. It makes more sense if we work together."

Inwardly, Shaunna groaned. This was not working out as planned. Not at all.

"And you will stay for dinner. You and Lanie." Maria

didn't even bother posing it as a question to Tyler, simpl
made the statement.

"We will stay," Tyler said, and started for the doo
"Ready, Shaunna?"

"Ready," she said, giving in. And when she saw Maria'
grin, Shaunna knew keeping her relationship with Tyl
strictly business wasn't going to be easy.

It took them an hour to clean the office, and Tyler er
joyed every minute of that time. He could tell Shaunna wa
trying to keep her distance, and he let her, at least to
point. Three days ago, he'd realized he was in love wit
her, and he knew she was attracted to him. The way sh
was acting, he could only assume she was fighting thos
feelings. So he wasn't going to rush things. By doing h
bookkeeping, he had an excuse to spend time with her. An
Maria, bless her soul, was giving him even more excuse

Once they had the desk cleared off, Shaunna brought hi
the statements he needed, along with the pile of unpaid bil
and her bank book. He suspected she would have escape
then if he hadn't asked her to stay while he looked ove
everything…just in case he had any questions. He coul
tell the idea didn't please her. What he couldn't understar
was why she seemed so nervous.

And then he began to understand.

She hadn't been keeping up her bank book. The ban
statements showed that checks had been written and cashe
but nothing had been written down. No amounts. No date
And no payee. Finally, he looked up. "How do you kno
who's been paid and who hasn't?"

"Well…" She avoided his gaze. "I don't, I guess."

"You haven't written it down anywhere?"

She shook her head again, and he began flipping bac
through her bank book.

"When did you last balance your checking account?"

"I…"

He looked up, and she shrugged.

Her attitude surprised him. He knew if he asked her a question about any of her horses, she would know exactly what had been done to or for that horse in the past six months. He'd heard her explain to others, in great detail, feeding schedules, training routines and medical needs. Her lackadaisical attitude about her finances simply didn't make sense. "Do you have any idea how much money you make each month? Or pay out?"

Tyler watched her chew on her lower lip. Again, she merely shook her head.

Her response was beyond his comprehension. "How in heaven's name can you run a business if you don't know your income and outgo?"

The moment he asked the question, he knew he'd said something wrong. Shaking her head, she backed toward the door. "I've got to go," she said. "I…I need to check on the horses."

She vanished from the office so quickly, he didn't have a chance to stop her. And by the time he did act, she truly had vanished. Looking up and down the aisle of the barn and calling her name produced no results. He was heading for the other barn when he ran into Maria.

"Ah, good, I find you," she said, huffing as she caught up with him. "You like rice?" she asked.

"Sure, rice is fine." He kept glancing around the stable yard. "Have you seen Shaunna?"

"I thought she was with you."

"She was, but I said something that evidently upset her, and she just disappeared."

Maria's frown was immediate. "You say something not so nice?"

"I was upset with her bookkeeping practices...or lack of bookkeeping." He kept looking around for Shaunna, half-expecting to see her ride off into the sunset even though it was too early for the sun to set.

"Shaunna, she has trouble with numbers." Maria tapped her head. "They get mixed up for her."

Realization dawned on him. "She has numeric dyslexia?"

"*Sí,* I think that was what Miss Betsy called it. For Shaunna, the numbers get all mixed up. When Miss Betsy alive, no problem. She always take care of everything, but after Miss Betsy die, Shaunna gets very upset. She tries her best, but she can't do it. I try, but I can't do it, either. So we hire a bookkeeper, and she stays for a while, then goes. So we hire another one, but this one not so honest. After that, Shaunna says no more. But she can't do it. That's why I'm glad she hires you." Maria grinned. "Shaunna, she needs you in many ways, I think."

"I hope so." He knew he needed her. "But I get the feeling she's trying to avoid me."

"She is afraid you will run off and leave her like the others did."

"I'm not going to run off and leave her."

"No, I think not."

"And I'm not going to steal from her."

"Steal money, she'll get over it. Steal heart..." Maria shook her head. "That is not good." She looked toward the smaller barn. "He kept his horse there. Very good-looking man. Even I thought so. But not good inside." Maria tapped her ample chest just above her breasts. "Poor Shaunna, she really liked him. I think she was maybe twenty then. I know how she feels. I was only eighteen when I get fooled by a man. For me, my foolishness gives me my Anna, and I'm not sorry about that. For Shaunna, she only gets a broken heart.''

"I don't want to break her heart," Tyler said.

"I think you won't. I've watched you with your little girl. You are a good man. Shaunna, she needs someone like you.''

"But how do I convince her of that?"

"We will find a way." Maria smiled, her round face growing rounder. "I go fix rice now. Dinner be ready at six.''

Shaunna knew taking off had been stupid, but her reaction to Tyler's criticism had been instinctive. Although it had been years since she'd been chastised for her incompetence, the tone of Tyler's voice had brought back memories. She'd tried as a child to do her math homework. She'd worked as hard or harder than any other child in her classroom, but the answer she produced never resembled the answers the teacher was looking for. And when her father found her papers with all the red marks, the result for her was always the same. He would yell and the belt would come off and then came the beatings, made worse if he happened to be drinking that particular day. Which was just about every day.

Intellectually, Shaunna knew Tyler wouldn't whip her. And since those childhood days, she'd learned that her problem with numbers wasn't due to laziness or stupidity. At least, that was what the woman who tested her had said. Certain connections simply didn't occur in her brain. It was no big deal, both the woman and Betsy had said. They'd also said that she'd obviously learned to function with the handicap.

But she hadn't learned how to admit it to others.

Shaunna found a hammer and nails and headed out the

back of the small barn to check paddock fences. Anything to keep her busy and away from Tyler. She made it to the first fence before he found her.

"So there you are," Tyler said, coming around the side of the barn.

Shaunna watched him walk toward her, the sun glinting off his hair. From his expression, she knew he wasn't happy with her. She couldn't say she was happy with herself. She couldn't even explain her behavior, simply held up the hammer in her hand. "I thought I'd better check the fences."

"Why didn't you tell me?"

She pretended she didn't understand. "I just thought of it."

"Maria told me."

That was all he said, and she let her arm fall back to her side. Pretending she didn't know what he was talking about wasn't going to work. And when he stopped directly in front of her, she sighed. "I did tell you. At least, I tried to. I told you I was no good with numbers, that what was easy for you wasn't for me. I told you we were totally opposite."

"We are definitely different." He touched her chin with the tips of his fingers, tilting her head up. "But it doesn't matter, Shaunna. You can do things I can't do."

"I can't make change. Not even for a dollar. That's why I have people make their own change."

"And I can't talk to horses." He smiled. "We each have our strengths and weaknesses."

The look in his eyes was warm and tempting, his touch so gentle she almost believed him. "People don't need to talk to horses to survive. They do need to know how to balance a checkbook."

"Or they hire someone who can. I'm here for you now.

Shaunna. And I'm not going to disappear or skim off your money." But he did skim his mouth over hers.

She trembled, her knees growing weak. "Oh, Tyler..."

"Shh."

He kissed her again, the touch of his lips light and gentle. Merely a promise. A teasing prelude that made her want more. And without truly thinking, she asked for more, reaching out to him and touching his shoulders, her fingers curling into the soft cotton of his shirt.

"Oh, yes," he murmured on a sigh and deepened the kiss, sending tingling messages through her bloodstream and awakening a desire she'd tried to deny.

Oh, yes, her mind echoed, the admission coming from deep within her soul. This was what she'd wanted. The tension and nervousness all had a meaning. Her body had warned her that ignoring her feelings wouldn't work. Logic had no meaning in the world of emotions. Words might convey one message; a racing pulse delivered another.

She should have listened more closely.

Now she gave in, savoring the taste of him and the feel of his hands, his touch never confining. She could run if she wanted to. Bolt for freedom. But she stayed where she was, in his arms, pressing her body against his. Curves molded to angles, and she felt her breasts flatten and the hardness of his desire press against her. Images raced through her mind—of them naked, their limbs entwined and his body becoming a part of hers. The idea stole her breath away, the heat of her passion burning through her.

Only when Tyler broke off the kiss did she suck in the air she needed, the sound almost a gasp. His breathing was no more even, and the way he was looking at her, she knew he was equally shaken. In his eyes was desire, and she knew what his body was telling her. This was not going to be strictly a business arrangement.

He spoke first, but didn't release his hold on her, and there was a huskiness to his voice that hadn't been present before. "I think we need to talk."

She didn't want to talk. She wanted to make love with him, to forget her fears and enjoy the sensations he could so easily arouse in her. Yet she knew he was right; something needed to be said. Nevertheless, she only nodded.

"I want to make love with you," he said. "I think you know that."

Again, she could only nod.

"And I think you want to make love with me. But I don't want to rush things. I don't want you thinking I'm hopping from one woman to the next, that I only want your body."

She wasn't sure what to think. All she could do was stare up into his eyes and wait for what he would say next.

"I think we need to take this slowly. Get to know each other better."

She didn't want to admit he was right, yet she knew he was. Once more, she gave a nod.

"Good." He smiled and gave her a quick hug. Then he released his hold and stretched out a hand. "Come on. Let's go tackle those books."

Chapter Twelve

Shaunna wasn't sure if she was pleased or disappointed to discover Tyler was true to his word. He was taking things slowly, letting her get to know him. He might surprise her with a quick kiss, but he never let it go too far, and she found she was the one wishing he didn't have so much self-control.

Nevertheless, she didn't tell him she wanted more. She feared she was in love with him, and knew that was foolish. He'd told her once that he didn't believe in love. For her sake, it seemed safest not to take their relationship to the next step.

The weekend of the horse show came quickly. For two weeks, Lanie had ridden Magic every day, taking lessons and trail rides with Patti and Bobby. Other than minor problems, the horse acted fine, and when the time for a final decision came, neither Shaunna nor Tyler could think of a reason why Lanie shouldn't show the horse.

The day of the show, Lanie was nervous, which Shaunna had expected. Once they were at the show grounds and settled in, Shaunna talked to Bobby and Patti, asking them to help Lanie. Most of all, she encouraged the three children to keep their horses relaxed and calm. "It should be a fun time for you and your horses," she told each of the ten-year-olds. "You stay relaxed and so will your horse."

It wasn't until the three were in the warm-up ring that Shaunna realized how tense and nervous Tyler was. From outside the arena, he kept shouting instructions to Lanie. Finally, Shaunna went over to his side.

"Relax, Dad," Shaunna told him, keeping a watchful eye on Bobby as he showed off for Lanie. "She'll do fine. Just think of this as a learning experience for the two of them."

"It's a learning experience for me." For a moment, his gaze left Lanie to take in the others in the arena. "Do you realize a year ago I didn't know one end of a horse from the other. Didn't own a Stetson." He tapped the one on his head. "Or boots."

Shaunna glanced down at his Tony Lama boots, their shine a contrast to her scuffed pair. He also had on denims and a Western shirt. He almost looked like a cowboy.

Almost.

"We haven't gotten you up on a horse yet," she said.

"One step at a time, thank you."

Shaunna watched a stylish young rider cut in front of Lanie.

"What the—" Tyler started to yell.

Shaunna stopped him with a hand on his arm. "Don't get upset. She's got to learn to deal with things like that. Look, she's doing fine."

Tyler grumbled his response. "Who does that kid think she is anyway?"

"That's Marina Gray. Her father is a big-shot lawyer who gives her the best money can buy. He sees to it that his daughter gets private lessons, has her riding outfits made specially for her, and he's sent the horse she's on to a professional trainer for six months. She wins most of her classes and has been led to believe that she's better than everyone else.''

"Lanie shouldn't have to compete against someone like that." He kept watching the girl.

"Lanie's got to learn to deal with people like Marina. In horse shows, you'll find the same types you have in life. There are the braggarts, the ones who demand to be the center of attention. The pushy, who wouldn't hesitate to get between you and the judge. And the snobs, who own the most expensive or better-bred horses and let you know you're not in their class. Then there are the quiet ones, some who are self-assured and will enter the arena and surprise everyone by riding off with the prize, and others who will come and go and you'll never remember them, and neither will the judge. Probably the worst, however, are the fools, those riders who do everything wrong, and you hurt for them, but they're not even aware that they're doing things wrong.''

"And will that be Lanie?"

"No, that won't be Lanie." She patted his arm, wishing she could convey how pleased he should be with his daughter. "Look at her. She didn't let Marina bother her. She's going around just as calm and steady as an old pro. She'll do fine, Tyler. The one I'm worried about is you.''

He gave her a quick glance. "Me? Why are you worried about me?''

"Don't be too critical of her. Whether she places or not shouldn't matter. That she gives her best is all you should ask.''

He hesitated and finally smiled. "Message received. You're right. I'm the one who's acting like the fool. All

my yelling will do is upset Lanie, and it really doesn't
matter how she does as long as she tries." He studied the
riders for a moment. "But you know, since Lanie's had
you for a teacher, I have a feeling she'll give that Marina
a run for her money. That lawyer might think he has the
best trainer that money can buy, but he's wrong. Lanie has
her. You just don't realize how much you should be charging us for your expertise."

Shaunna chuckled at the idea but was pleased he thought
so. "I'm lucky you're not charging me what you're worth
to straighten out my books."

"We're getting there. I showed you that balance sheet
yesterday. Things are looking good."

He'd showed her, which had proven to her that he really
didn't understand her inability to make sense of numbers.
If he said the stable was making a nice profit, that was
great, but the numbers on the page had meant nothing to
her. Still, it was nice to know she didn't have to worry
about going bankrupt, that all of her creditors had been
paid, and she could actually spend some money for the
repairs she'd wanted to make.

"What's she doing now?"

Tyler was looking at Lanie, and Shaunna followed his
gaze. The little girl had taken Magic into the center of the
arena and was backing him up. "She's just practicing what
she has to do in there." Shaunna pointed toward the main
show arena, where the class in progress was backing their
horses for the judge. And from where the judge was in the
lineup, Shaunna knew they didn't have much more time
until Lanie and the others would be entering for their class.
"I'm going to go over and talk to the kids. Will you be all
right?"

"Not until this is over."

She smiled and left him, and Tyler watched Shaunna

move down near the gate. With a wave of her hand, she brought her three riders to her. Lanie leaned over Magic's shoulder so she could hear Shaunna, and Magic rubbed his face against Shaunna's arm.

In a way, Tyler was jealous of the closeness between Lanie and Shaunna. The girl lived and breathed horses twenty-four hours a day, adored Maria and idolized Shaunna. He knew, from what Lanie had said, she'd like to move in with Shaunna and live at the stable.

Tyler had to admit he wouldn't mind moving in with Shaunna himself, but he didn't want to make the suggestion yet. For one thing, he wanted to make sure he had some financial security. Which seemed to be happening. Shaunna's books, as disorganized as they were, weren't taking all of his time, and he'd already lined up several other clients. Going into business for himself was becoming a reality, and he liked being his own boss. Losing his job had been the best thing to happen to him…except for meeting Shaunna.

He'd told her he would give her time to get to know him, and he would, if it killed him. He hadn't, however, expected it to be so difficult to keep his hands off her. Every time he gave her a kiss, he wanted to take it farther and make love with her. For a man who hadn't had any problems restricting his sexual desires around Alicia, he was discovering that self-control around Shaunna was almost nonexistent.

The days he worked at the stable were a mixture of pleasure and pain. There was her smile in the morning when he first arrived at the stable and joined Shaunna for a cup of coffee. It warmed him to the core. And her laughter drifting through the barn as he worked on the balance sheets. He'd often stop what he was doing to get up and see what she was laughing at. And always the sound of her

voice, so husky and soothing, tempted him. More than once
he'd forgotten the column of numbers he was adding,
closed his eyes and pictured her softly murmuring endear-
ments as they made love.

Even watching her on a horse had him thinking erotic
thoughts. For a man who'd once figured celibacy was no
big deal, his inability to block out images of lovemaking
had him frustrated. He needed Shaunna, physically and
emotionally, as he'd never needed a woman before, not
even Barbara. Around Shaunna he felt whole, and when he
drove away in the evening, he felt he was leaving a part of
himself behind.

He knew he wouldn't be able to hold back from express-
ing his feelings for long, and he knew he had to tell her
about Lanie. Not that he supposed it would matter to her.
So far, however, the timing just hadn't seemed right.

The riders in the show arena had been lined up for some
time. Suddenly, the announcer began calling off the places.
He saw Shaunna glance that way and Lanie straighten in
the saddle. Shaunna said a few more words to Patti, Bobby
and Lanie, then gave each of them a pat on the leg. It was
then that Lanie looked his way and tipped her hat.

He tipped his hat back and swallowed hard. This was the
moment.

When Shaunna came back to his side, they found spots
along the outside of the main arena where they could watch
the event. Eleven horses entered at a slow trot, Marina leading the group, her outfit the flashiest and her attitude clearly
superior. A couple of horses back, Patti followed, then
came Lanie with Bobby behind her. It didn't seem fair to
Tyler that Lanie had to compete against someone like Marina or against her friends, yet he had to admit she looked
as competent as the other ten in the ring. And he wasn't
hesitant to say so. "She looks good."

"I told you, she is good." Shaunna leaned against the railing. "Of course, I have to be impartial. With three of my kids in there, I can't be hoping one wins over the others."

Yet her smile told him she was, and he leaned close and kissed her cheek. Immediately, she looked at him, and he smiled. "For luck."

She grinned back. "Let's hope it works."

The judge probably didn't take any longer with Lanie's class than he had with any of the others, but for Tyler, it seemed the man was taking an eternity to make a decision. Around and around the arena, the horses and riders walked, trotted and loped, first in one direction, then in the other. Some, in Tyler's opinion, looked better than others, and a couple of the horses, including Bobby's, took up the wrong lead the second time they went into a lope. What made one horse or one rider better than another, however, was difficult for Tyler to see.

In his estimation, Lanie was the best. She looked so poised and mature, sitting so straight in the saddle. And Magic moved with the ease of a horse long accustomed to life under the saddle, his tail relaxed, his head low and his ears perked forward. The mahogany coat that had once been dull and matted with dung now gleamed with a luster of good health and care. Ribs no longer showing, the well-fed Mustang's body rippled with muscle.

Tyler smiled as Lanie rode past, and she smiled at him.

And then, all hell broke loose.

At first, Tyler wasn't sure what happened. All he saw was the horse closest to him shoot up in the air, rearing and bucking. Then he heard a scream, followed by more yelling, some from the riders and some from the parents. One horse bolted, its rider falling off.

From beside him, Shaunna slipped into the arena right in front of the riderless horse. She caught it by the reins, taking a few steps with it and using her hands to guide it into circling her. As it made a loop around her, she talked in soothing tones, and slowly the horse lost its look of fear. Tyler knew Shaunna had once again worked her magic.

Only then did he realize it was Marina standing in the middle of the arena, her flashy outfit covered with dust, her hat off and tears running down her face. Shaunna walked the horse back to the girl and handed her the reins, then quickly returned to Tyler's side. Once there, she turned to him. "Lanie okay?"

"She's fine." He'd seen Magic break stride and Lanie grab for the saddle horn to keep her balance, but as quickly as he'd reacted, the Mustang had settled down, coming to a stop and standing quietly while Shaunna caught the frightened horse. Even now, Magic only shifted weight and swished his tail.

Shaunna checked on Bobby and Patti, giving a sigh when she found both of them in the saddle, their horses relatively quiet. "Good," she said. "Those practice times paid off."

"What happened anyway?" Tyler had no idea.

"I think a kid threw something into the arena. There." She pointed toward the long, brightly colored, snakelike object the ring steward was picking up. "Looks like a Slinky toy."

"And you practiced for that?"

"With Magic as spooked as he was about whips and anything waving in the air, I felt we had to, for Lanie's sake, and I just included Bobby and Patti in the lessons, too. Now I'm glad I did."

"Our Marina doesn't look too happy." Tyler watched the girl remount her horse, tears still streaming down her cheeks.

"Sometimes the pampered life is too safe. If you're not ready for surprises, they can throw you. Now we'll see what kind of rider she is."

In a moment, it was all too clear. Marina jerked on her horse's reins, pulling viciously on his mouth. And though Tyler couldn't hear the words the girl was saying, the way she kicked her horse showed her anger. Once again, the horse reared. This time, Marina stayed on, but as soon as the horse came down, she was off its back, jerking on the reins and dragging it toward the exit gate.

"And then there were ten," Shaunna said.

Once Marina and her horse had left the arena, the ring steward signaled for the remaining riders to take up a walk. The judge had the horses go twice around the arena, then asked the riders to line up.

The judge went from horse and rider to horse and rider, having each rider back up his or her horse, then return to the line. He said something to Lanie and Lanie answered. Tyler couldn't make out what she said, but she was smiling when the judge walked on.

Tyler held his breath when they began announcing the placings. They started with sixth place, and Bobby's name was called. Shaunna began clapping her hands and Tyler followed suit, knowing Bobby's mother and father were somewhere in the stands and probably as nervous as he was. As fifth and fourth places were called out, Tyler felt Shaunna move her hand, and he found he'd been holding it, squeezing her fingers. She gave him a smile as she shook the blood back into her fingertips.

And then the announcer called out Lanie's name along with Magic's, and Tyler realized she'd taken third and was riding away from the line to pick up her ribbon from the judge. Tyler was clapping and shouting and hooting. And when he looked at Shaunna, he knew what he had to do.

He lifted her off her feet and spun her around. Her hat fell off and she laughed at him. "Tyler, put me down."

"She won," he shouted. "She won!"

"I took third," Lanie yelled the moment she rode out of the ring. Waving the yellow ribbon in the air, she nudged Magic into a trot and headed in their direction. "And the judge said I'm very good and Magic is beautiful. He was really impressed with Magic for not getting spooked when that thing was thrown into the ring. And I beat Bobby, but I'm not really glad I did that." She glanced back into the arena. "And look, Patti took first. Isn't that wonderful? And that one girl fell off, and..."

She kept chattering, waving the yellow ribbon and grinning, and Tyler knew all the weeks of sitting by her bedside, praying she would live, and the months of frustration he'd endured, trying to overcome her anger, had been worth it. He couldn't have been prouder or happier. "You won," he said to her and didn't care that he truly was going to make a fool of himself.

He hugged the horse.

Lanie was still wound up when they returned to the stable and her mood was being picked up by Magic. When they led the horse out of the trailer, he was hot and sweaty. Too hot to put up. "Walk him about for a while," Shaunna told Lanie, knowing the exercise would calm the girl, as well.

"Can I let him eat some grass?" Lanie asked, glancing toward the lush green lawn in front of the house that was off-limits to horses. "As a special treat?"

"Okay." Shaunna knew Magic deserved a special treat after his behavior that day. "But just this one time, or Maria will really get mad at us."

She watched the girl lead the horse toward the lawn, then

she headed for the barn. Tyler was unloading the tack, getting everything out of the trailer and back where it belonged. Bobby and Patti were putting up their horses, their parents helping them. Shaunna went to each child, giving words of praise and making sure the horses were properly cared for. Only after Bobby and Patti and their parents had left did Shaunna go looking for Tyler.

She found him outside Magic's stall, tacking up the yellow ribbon Lanie had won. "Are we feeling pretty proud, Dad?" Shaunna asked, standing back and watching him.

"Proud as can be." He stepped back to view his handiwork, then walked over to her side. "Thanks."

"Don't thank me. Lanie did the work."

"Yeah, and you did nothing." He grinned and slipped an arm around her shoulders, giving her a squeeze. "Where is she anyway?"

"Still grazing Magic, I guess. Maybe we'd better check." Shaunna eased herself away from his embrace, surprised by the pain his hug had caused in her right shoulder. Walking toward the outside door, she rotated her arm, trying to find the spot where it hurt.

Just inside the barn, Tyler stopped her. "Something wrong?"

Again, Shaunna flexed her shoulder. "I guess I pulled a muscle or something when I grabbed that horse today. It's sore, but I don't think it's anything drastic."

"Let me see." He gently touched her shoulder, pressing against the muscle in various places.

When he hit the spot, she flinched. "That's it."

"We'll have to put some liniment on that." He turned her toward him, his expression serious. "You scared me to death, you know. That horse could have run you down."

"Horses don't intentionally run into people if they have

a choice, but as wild-eyed as he was, I wasn't sure he wouldn't try going through that fence."

"So you jumped in to stop him." He brushed his fingertips over her cheek. "What am I going to do with you?"

"I don't know." But she liked the way he was looking at her, all warm and caring.

"Just love you, I guess."

She swallowed hard. She wanted to believe he meant the words, but she was afraid to hope. "You don't believe in love, remember?"

"You're turning me into a believer."

"Oh, Tyler…"

He smiled. "Crazy, isn't it?"

What was crazier was the way her heart was racing and the expression on his face. "Are you going to kiss me or what?" she asked, certain she would have a heart attack if he didn't.

"I'm going to kiss you," he said, and did.

At first, the touch of his lips on hers was gentle, but within seconds, that changed to wild and passionate. Shaunna kissed him back, hugging him close and ignoring the pain in her shoulder. She kissed him and loved him and wanted to shout out her joy and weep her relief. He loved her…and she loved him. It was insane and unbelievable and absolutely wonderful.

She didn't want to stop kissing him and she didn't want to stop at a kiss. And when he slipped his tongue into her mouth and rubbed his hands over her body, drawing her hips even tighter against his, the hard pressure of his desire only echoed her own.

The sound of horses stomping flies had long ago faded into the background, her senses keyed only to the ragged rhythm of her breathing and the wild thud of her heart. *Just love you, I guess.* The words played over and over in her head.

He loved her.

And then Shaunna heard a small gasp.

It wasn't more than an intake of breath, but it pierced the melee of her emotions. Shaunna drew back from Tyler's embrace enough to glance toward the entrance to the barn. There stood Lanie, Magic just behind her. Wide-eyed, the girl stared at them.

Shaunna saw Lanie's chin tremble, and the girl closed her eyes as if trying to block out the sight of her father kissing someone. Tyler also saw her. Slowly, he straightened, keeping an arm around Shaunna but facing Lanie. "Honey?" he questioned. "Lanie?"

She opened her eyes, the tears forming.

"I thought you'd be happy about Shaunna and me."

"Happy?" Lanie shook her head, the tears sliding down her cheeks.

"I love Shaunna," Tyler said. "And I think she loves me."

"I was afraid this would happen."

"Why are you afraid?" Shaunna asked, confused by the girl's reaction.

"Because now he won't want me around. You two will get married and he'll make me go away."

Shaunna released her hold on Tyler and stepped toward the girl. "Lanie, of course he'll want you around. Why wouldn't he?"

"Why?" Lanie backed away, taking Magic with her. "Because he's not my real father."

Chapter Thirteen

"Oh, my God," Tyler gasped. "I didn't think you knew." He watched Lanie turn away from them and take off, pulling Magic with her.

"She's not your daughter?" Shaunna asked, looking back at him.

He could only shake his head. For in front of him, he saw Magic pull back on the lead rope, then rear. He heard Lanie cry out and watched the horse lift her from her feet as she clung to the rope. And then he saw the horse come down and Lanie fall to the ground. Magic's hooves came so close to Lanie's body that Tyler was sure the horse had hit her with his front feet. Then two of the stable dogs started barking, and Magic bolted, his lead rope flopping loosely in the air. When Lanie scrambled to her feet, Tyler knew she hadn't been touched by the horse.

It was then that he saw Chris Prescott's van pulling into the stable yard. Magic was running straight for it, and Lanie started after him, yelling for him to stop. Shaunna also took off, calling out a warning to Chris as the dogs kept barking and chasing the horse. All the while, standing where he was, his stomach twisting into a knot, Tyler watched, helplessly unable to do anything.

He knew the moment Chris realized what was happening. He heard the squeal of her brakes and the crunch of gravel as she tried to stop the van. There simply wasn't enough time. Horse and van were on a collision path, and with a thump, metal hit horseflesh. Then there were two screams, one from Lanie and one from Magic.

The horse's cry of pain cut through Tyler, and he could see the horse was down on his side, flailing the air with his feet. Then he realized Lanie was running straight for the horse. "No!" Tyler yelled, realizing the danger. "Lanie, don't!"

He also started running, heading for the spot where Magic was down. He knew he couldn't get there before Lanie did. Again, he yelled for her to stay back. But Lanie ignored him. In spite of the horse's thrashing legs and efforts to rise, she went directly to Magic's side.

Tyler held his breath as he watched her kneel beside the injured horse. One of those legs could hit her. The horse had no idea what he was doing. Tyler didn't want Lanie hurt. She might not be his flesh and blood, but he'd loved her as a baby and he loved her now.

Chris jumped out of the van, her face ashen as she stared at the horse and Lanie. "Oh, God, I'm so sorry," she kept saying.

Tyler ignored her and went directly to Lanie. Shaunna was holding the horse's head down, keeping him from flailing around and injuring himself more, but Tyler saw blood on Lanie's hand and started to pull her back. She resisted, her eyes filled with tears when she looked up at him. "He's hurt," she cried.

He realized then that the blood was coming from a gash

on Magic's side and not from Lanie, and he let her continue pressing her hand against Magic's torn flesh. He wasn't sure what else to do.

Tears ran down Lanie's cheeks and her words to the horse were choked. "It's all right, Magic," she kept saying over and over. "It's all right." Again, she looked up at him. "Don't let him die, Daddy. Please, don't let him die."

Her words tore at his heart. It was the first time she'd called him Daddy, and he knew he would promise her anything. "We're not going to let him die," he said, kneeling beside her and also trying to calm the horse.

"We need a rag," Shaunna said, still holding the horse still. "Something to stop the bleeding."

"Use my shirt." Even as he made the offer, he was on his feet, jerking it free from his jeans and popping buttons as he pulled it off.

Shaunna didn't hesitate but took the shirt, moving Lanie's hand just long enough to press the cloth over the gash on the horse's side.

Magic continued trying to rise to his feet, and Shaunna looked at Lanie. "Let's let him stand if he wants. You take the lead rope, and I'll hold the shirt in place."

Shaunna moved to the side so Magic would have room, and Chris stepped back, all the while continuing her apologies. "I just came back to get Jeffery's lunch pail," she said. "He left it here. I didn't see—"

Shaunna cut her off. "It wasn't your fault, Chris. It's okay. Go call the vet for me. Maria will get you the number. Tell him what happened. See if he can come out."

Tyler found himself wanting to help Magic in his struggle and didn't realize he was squeezing Lanie's shoulder, not until she winced and looked at him. Immediately, he released his hold. "Sorry."

Magic continued to struggle to rise to his feet, the whites

of his eyes showing his fear. "You can do it," Lanie said, using her hands and words to encourage him. "You can do it, boy."

Magic did do it, finally heaving himself to his feet. The moment he was upright, he began shaking. Still holding Tyler's shirt over the gash in the horse's side, Shaunna began checking his body, her hands moving swiftly. "Check that side," she ordered Tyler. "See if you feel any broken bones. Tell me if he flinches from your touch."

The horse did flinch when Tyler pressed against his left shoulder, and there was some bleeding from cuts in the horse's flesh. He relayed the information to Shaunna.

"Probably where he hit the ground on that side," she said. "Let's hope it's not broken." She looked at Lanie. "See if you can lead him a few steps. Don't force him. Just see if he can walk."

Holding on to the lead rope, Lanie stepped away from Magic, facing him as she did and putting a little tension on the rope. "Come on, boy," she said tentatively. "You can do it. Let's take a little walk."

At first, Tyler didn't think the horse would move. He'd never seen a horse shake as much as Magic was shaking. The horse's entire body seemed to be trembling, his head low and his eyes wide and full of fear. But Lanie kept urging him to follow her, and finally, Magic did take a step. A small one. Tentative and unsure. Then another, and another.

"Good," Shaunna said almost on a sigh.

From the house, Chris yelled to them. "The vet wants to talk to you, Shaunna. Can you come?"

Shaunna gave him a questioning look, and he knew what was needed. "I'll hold that in place," he said, moving around to Shaunna's side of the horse.

"Good. Just keep up enough pressure to stop the bleeding. I'll find out what's up."

She was gone at a run, and Tyler did as ordered, pressing his hands where Shaunna had had hers. Lanie continued speaking to Magic in soothing tones, and Tyler felt the horse give a deep sigh, then lean his head against Lanie's shoulder. He knew then that the bond between the horse and the child was as strong as any human bond, and he knew he would do anything to save Magic's life.

Chris returned to her van, talking incessantly. "He just came out of nowhere. I jammed on the brakes as soon as I saw him. I never expected a horse to be in the driveway. I—"

"It's all right," Lanie said, sounding far more mature than her ten years. "It's not your fault."

"It's no one's fault," Tyler said, not wanting Lanie to shoulder the responsibility, either.

"I shouldn't have jerked on his rope," Lanie said. "I scared him."

"You didn't mean to. You were upset." He ached for the child. She was the innocent victim, forced into a situation that was none of her making. If anyone was to blame, he was the one. "I didn't know you knew."

She nodded and looked away, and he took a deep breath. This wasn't the time to discuss Lanie's parentage—now they had to worry about Magic, take care of him—but they would have to deal with it soon. It was time for the silence to end. There would be no more secrets.

He heard Shaunna then. "The vet's on the way," she called. "He wants us to get Magic to his stall if we can, then get a blanket on him. He's worried about the horse going into shock."

"I'll get a blanket," Chris said. "You can use my horse's."

"Bring it to us," Shaunna ordered, reaching Magic's side. "I want to get it on him right away."

Working together, the three of them eased Magic toward his stall. Tyler kept pressure on the bleeding gash in the horse's side; Lanie urged Magic on; and Shaunna slipped the horse blanket over Magic's back as soon as Chris had brought it.

"I've got to get back home," Chris said, standing to the side as they led Magic into his stall. "I left Jeffery with a neighbor."

"Go on. There's nothing more you can do here," Shaunna said as she made sure the door to the outside paddock was closed.

"I really am sorry," Chris said to Lanie, then looked at Tyler. "I—I tried to stop."

"It's all right," he said, wishing she would leave. Simply listening to the panic in her voice made him edgy. On the other hand, Shaunna's calm efficiency soothed him.

"What do we do?" Lanie asked, looking at Shaunna.

"Just keep him quiet now." She moved closer to Magic's side, where Tyler continued holding his shirt against the gash. "Good," she said to him. "Bleeding's almost stopped. Keep the pressure on."

Shaunna stepped back and studied the scene. She liked the way Tyler had stepped in, calmly doing everything she'd asked him to do. His attitude was helping Lanie and, in turn, was helping Magic.

"He got scared," Shaunna said to Lanie. "But I don't think he's hurt too badly. Just keep talking to him, let him know he's all right. Don't forget, he's a Mustang. He's grown up with danger all around him. He's stronger than those pampered horses that never have to really run from a predator, just think they do."

As Lanie continued stroking Magic and crooning to him,

Shaunna could see the horse start to relax. His eyes grew softer and the shaking stopped. He nuzzled Lanie's chest, lipping her shirt, then blowing through his nostrils.

The horse was growing calmer, and so was Lanie. *He's not my real father.* The words had been a shock to Shaunna, but thinking it over, she found it all made sense.

Now she understood the lack of similarity between father and daughter, understood why Lanie always called him Tyler and why Tyler never referred to Lanie as his daughter. Except, Shaunna realized, he'd been as surprised by Lanie's statement as she had.

He hadn't known that Lanie knew.

There were so many questions she wanted to ask. For weeks, she'd classified him with her father, had thought he'd deserted his child. But if Lanie wasn't his...?

Shaunna heard the crunch of tires on the gravel in the yard. "That should be the vet," she said, and left Magic's stall. "I'll go get him."

It took an hour for the veterinarian to clean the gash on Magic's side, stitch it and tend to all the other abrasions on the horse. He took Magic's temperature, listened to his heart and the sounds of his stomach, then spoke to Lanie. "You're a lucky girl. Other than that cut, I don't think there's anything seriously wrong with him." His gaze switched to Shaunna. "You should watch him for shock, however. If he shows any signs, it could mean internal bleeding. In that case, give me a call right away."

"How long before we'll know if he's going to be all right or not?" Tyler asked.

The vet glanced his way. "I'd say twenty-four hours. If he doesn't show any signs of discomfort, bleeding or shock in that time, you'll be out of the woods."

* * *

Tyler accompanied the vet back to his truck and thanked him for coming so quickly. After watching him drive away, Tyler returned to the barn. One crisis seemed to have been resolved. Another needed to be tackled.

Slowly, he walked down the aisle toward Magic's stall. He wasn't sure how to bring up the subject or what to say. Lanie knew, but how much did she know? "How's the old boy doing?" he asked when he reached Magic's stall.

"He's doing good," Lanie said, still fussing over the horse, combing her fingers through his mane and rubbing her hands over his good shoulder and chest. "Shaunna went to get some chairs. She said she'll set them up right where you are."

He looked around him, then back at Lanie. "Do I take it you plan on spending the night out here with him?"

Lanie looked at him seriously. "I can't leave him. You didn't leave me, did you, when I was in the hospital? They said you didn't. They said you stayed right by my side."

"No, I didn't leave you, Lanie, and if you want to spend the night out here with Magic, then we'll stay."

"You'll stay with me?"

"Of course. Because, no matter what you think, you *are* my daughter."

"I am?" She looked confused. "But Mommy said I wasn't."

"Well, maybe someone else was your father, but you're my daughter in every other way. So come here and give your daddy a hug."

He opened his arms, hoping Lanie would accept his love. For a moment, she simply stared at him, then slowly she walked into his embrace, wrapping her arms around him.

He knelt and held her close, feeling the tears well up in his eyes, but he didn't care. For the first time in years, his child was hugging him. As an infant, she'd wrapped her tiny fingers around his, and they'd been united. He'd loved her as he'd loved no other. And then she'd been torn from him.

He felt the shudder that went through Lanie and knew she was also crying. "How long have you known?" he asked softly.

"A long time." She sniffed, her voice cracking. "I got mad at Mommy one day and told her I was going to run away and live with you, and she said you weren't my real daddy and that you didn't want me."

"She shouldn't have told you that. I always wanted you."

Lanie pulled back slightly and looked at him with a frown. "Then how come you never came to see me?"

"Because your mother wanted it that way. She said it would be best if I was completely out of your life. And it hurt too much to see you and know you weren't mine anymore."

"I've got your name."

"Yes."

He saw Shaunna then, standing nearby, holding three folding chairs. He hadn't heard her approach and had no idea how much she'd overheard. He was glad she was there.

"Do you know what 'having an affair' means?" he asked Lanie.

She scowled at him. "Jeez, Daddy, what do you think I am, a child?"

Tyler decided she knew far more than he'd ever given her credit for. "Well, your mother had an affair while she and I were married. Only I didn't know she was having this affair, and when you were born, I thought you were my baby."

"Is that why I have your name?"

"That's one reason." He wouldn't go into the legal details.

"So how did you find out I wasn't yours?"

"Well, when you were almost six months old, you had to have an operation for a hernia. It was nothing major, still, I decided I'd be a good father and let the doctor know if he needed any blood for you, I'd be glad to donate some. But he said I couldn't, that my blood was too different from yours."

And he'd been shocked.

"Was it different because I wasn't yours?"

"Right."

"Was George my daddy?"

"No. George wasn't your daddy, either." He looked at Shaunna. "Your mother had the affair with someone else, someone who was also married. He'd told her he wouldn't marry her, but I think she thought he might after she got a divorce from me. I think she felt once he knew you were his baby, that he'd change his mind. At least, that's what she told me. But I guess it didn't matter to him because he never did marry her."

"Did it make you angry?" Lanie asked. "I mean, what Mommy did?"

"Yes," he said flatly. "It made me very angry."

Shaunna could imagine his feelings. He'd been cheated on by his wife and had just learned that the child he'd thought was his was another man's. That he'd walked away, had left his child—who wasn't his child—was beginning to make sense. His situation was in no way like her own. He was not like her father at all.

"I'd be angry, too," Lanie said very seriously.

"I think you have been angry. Haven't you?" Lanie hesitated a moment, then nodded, and Tyler drew her closer again. "You've had a right to be angry. We haven't treated you very well. Not your mother or me. None of this was your fault. You didn't have any say in it. I should have come and seen you while you were growing up.''

"Mommy said you hated me, that you hated her.''

"I didn't hate you,'' he said. "I never hated you. In fact, I missed you.''

"Then how come you didn't want me after the accident?''

He leaned back, frowning. "Who told you that?''

"I heard you talking to the doctor. You said he was crazy, that you couldn't take on a child.''

"What I meant...'' He looked at Lanie, then at Shaunna, then back at Lanie. "I didn't have any experience with children. How was I supposed to take care of a nine-and-a-half-year-old? I didn't have the slightest idea.''

Somehow he'd learned.

"I heard them tell you that you had to take me. They didn't give you a choice.''

Shaunna could tell that Lanie still didn't understand, and she felt it was time to say something. "Lanie, I don't think anyone makes your dad do anything he doesn't want to do. He had choices. He could have told everyone that you weren't his child. As he said, a blood test already proved that. There are other tests, too. He could have had you sent to a foster home. But instead, he never told anyone that you weren't his daughter, didn't even give a hint to anyone that you weren't, and he made a home for you even when he wasn't sure how to handle a daughter...especially a very angry daughter. And he made sure that your horse was helped because he knew it would help you. And he almost got married just because he thought it would be good for you to have a mother.''

Lanie's gaze was troubled. "But I'm not really his, and

f you two get married, you're not going to want me around.''

"Who says we wouldn't?" she asked. "Think of adopted children. They're not related to the people who adopt them, but their parents love them.''

"So does that mean you'll marry me?" Tyler asked, looking directly at Shaunna.

She hadn't thought of that when she'd responded to Lanie or considered the fact that Tyler hadn't asked. But the expression on his face gave her hope. "Depends on if you're asking.''

"What do you think?" he asked Lanie. "Should we marry her?''

"I sure like her a lot more than Ah-lee-sha.''

"So do I." He grinned and stood, still resting a hand on Lanie's shoulder. "Guess it's up to you, Shaunna. Here you have a child who is loving, caring and knows a heck of a lot more about horses than her dad." He presented Lanie by nudging her slightly toward Shaunna. "And a man who didn't think he wanted to fall in love again, but who's discovered he couldn't help himself.''

"So will you marry him?" Lanie asked, peering up at her.

Shaunna wanted to say yes, but she had her own fears. "I'm afraid I wouldn't be a very good mother.''

"Why not?" Tyler lifted his eyebrows in question.

"Because I don't know how to be one.''

"What's there to know?" Lanie asked plaintively, and Shaunna knew she had to explain to the child.

"How to act like a mother. How to love. I never learned that as a child. At least, not from my mother. She didn't want me, didn't want any children. I was an accident and a nuisance in her life. She was always telling me she couldn't wait until I grew up. I have no idea what most children experience with their parents. Have no idea how I'll act.''

"Oh, Shaunna." Tyler stepped away from Lanie, going to her. "Don't you realize you've been playing mother to everyone at this stable? Especially to your riding students. With them, you do everything a mother does. You encourage them when they need encouragement. Give them hugs when they're sad. I've seen it. And you discipline with compassion and understanding. Maybe you didn't learn how from your parents, but somewhere along the way, you learned.''

He cradled her head in his hands and made her face him. "Hey, I've been learning how to be a father from you. You're the one who's taught me how to listen to Lanie, to give in when necessary and to stand firm when needed." He paused and cocked his head. "So, what do you say? Will you marry me? Become Lanie's mother?''

How could she say no to this man? She hadn't been able to since the first time he'd called her. She hadn't had room for Lanie's horse in her stable, but Magic had become part of her family of horses. She hadn't wanted to care about him as a man, yet he'd wedged his way into her heart.

"I guess..." She smiled. "I guess I say yes."

Epilogue

Lanie decided Tyler and Shaunna's wedding was exactly what she wanted when she grew up. Shaunna had let her help plan it, and Maria had let her give a hand with the cooking. When Shaunna asked her to be the maid of honor, Lanie had eagerly said yes.

They decided to hold the wedding on the first weekend in October, and they invited everyone from the stable and all of Tyler's family and friends. Even Anna, Maria's daughter, came back that weekend so she could be a part of the festivities. Lanie decided she really liked her and maybe, when she grew up, she'd go to college, too.

The ceremony itself was held in the large arena, and everyone who came stood around the railing and watched. The preacher stood in the middle of the arena on the mounting block, so he was up off the dirt and high enough that he could be seen. And Tyler actually agreed to be on horseback, which Lanie thought was really neat, even though, before the wedding, he kept saying he had to be crazy. So all four of them—Shaunna and Tyler, Tyler's older brother, who was best man, and Lanie—were on horseback, and Lanie thought that was neat, too. She couldn't wait to see the pictures.

During the ceremony, Magic kept nodding his head as if he understood what the preacher was saying. Lanie kept patting him to keep him quiet while she watched Shaunna, who looked absolutely beautiful in the white cotton dress Maria had made for her. And every so often, Lanie glanced Tyler's way and grinned. Tyler looked so worried every time his horse moved. He also looked very distinguished in his Western-style tuxedo. He was the most handsome man alive, Lanie decided. Even better-looking than a movie star.

As the preacher rambled on and on about being true to each other, Lanie knew he was wasting his breath. Gads, every time she turned around, they were kissing. Lanie couldn't imagine them not being in love.

The preacher nodded at her, and she knew it was time for her to give the ring in her pocket to Shaunna. For a moment, she panicked when she put her hand in the pocket and couldn't find it, but then she touched the gold ring and sighed, grinning as she handed it to Shaunna.

Magic was getting restless by the time Shaunna and Tyler finished their vows, but she calmed him down enough so she could participate in the ending. That's when Tyler asked her to move over between them and all three of them joined hands. He'd said he wanted everyone to know they were a family. So Lanie gripped Shaunna's hand with her left and Tyler's in her right, and they lifted their arms so all could see, and Lanie knew she was going to cry.

And if Bobby saw her, he'd tease her something awful. But she didn't care. He could tease her all he wanted. What did he know? He was just a boy. He wouldn't understand how wonderful it was that now she had a daddy and also a mommy. He didn't know anything, but she did.

They were a family now...forever.

* * * * *

SILHOUETTE BOOKS
is proud to announce the arrival of

THE BABY OF THE MONTH CLUB:

the latest installment of author
Marie Ferrarella's
popular miniseries.

When pregnant Juliette St. Claire met Gabriel Saldana than she discovered he wasn't the struggling artist he claimed to be. An undercover agent, Gabriel had been sent to Juliette's gallery to nab his prime suspect: Juliette herself. But when he discovered her innocence, would he win back Juliette's heart and convince her that he was the daddy her baby needed?

Don't miss Juliette's induction into
THE BABY OF THE MONTH CLUB
in September 1999.

Available at your favorite retail outlet.

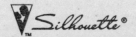

If you enjoyed what you just read,
then we've got an offer you can't resist!

Take 2 bestselling
love stories FREE!

Plus get a FREE surprise gift!

Clip this page and mail it to Silhouette Reader Service™

IN U.S.A.	**IN CANADA**
3010 Walden Ave.	P.O. Box 609
P.O. Box 1867	Fort Erie, Ontario
Buffalo, N.Y. 14240-1867	L2A 5X3

YES! Please send me 2 free Silhouette Romance® novels and my free surprise gift. Then send me 6 brand-new novels every month, which I will receive months before they're available in stores. In the U.S.A., bill me at the bargain price of $2.90 plus 25¢ delivery per book and applicable sales tax, if any*. In Canada, bill me at the bargain price of $3.25 plus 25¢ delivery per book and applicable taxes**. That's the complete price and a savings of over 10% off the cover prices—what a great deal! I understand that accepting the 2 free books and gift places me under no obligation ever to buy any books. I can always return a shipment and cancel at any time. Even if I never buy another book from Silhouette, the 2 free books and gift are mine to keep forever. So why not take us up on our invitation. You'll be glad you did!

215 SEN CNE7
315 SEN CNE9

Name	(PLEASE PRINT)	
Address	Apt.#	
City	State/Prov.	Zip/Postal Code

* Terms and prices subject to change without notice. Sales tax applicable in N.Y.
** Canadian residents will be charged applicable provincial taxes and GST.
All orders subject to approval. Offer limited to one per household.
® are registered trademarks of Harlequin Enterprises Limited.

SROM99   ©1998 Harlequin Enterprises Limited

Coming this September 1999
from SILHOUETTE BOOKS
and bestselling author

RACHEL LEE

CONARD COUNTY:

Boots & Badges

Alicia Dreyfus—a desperate woman on the run—
is about to discover that she *can* come home
again...to Conard County. Along the way she
meets the man of her dreams—and brings together
three other couples, whose love blossoms beneath
the bold Wyoming sky.

Enjoy four complete, **brand-new** stories in one
extraordinary volume.

Available at your favorite retail outlet.

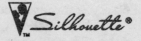

Silhouette ROMANCE™

VIRGIN BRIDES

Your favorite authors tell more heartwarming stories of lovely brides who discover love... for the first time....

July 1999 GLASS SLIPPER BRIDE
Arlene James (SR #1379)

Bodyguard Jack Keller had to protect innocent Jillian Waltham—day and night. But when his assignment became a matter of temporary marriage, would Jack's hardened heart need protection...from Jillian, his glass slipper bride?

September 1999 MARRIED TO THE SHEIK
Carol Grace (SR #1391)

Assistant Emily Claybourne secretly loved her boss, and now Sheik Ben Ali had finally asked her to marry him! But Ben was only interested in a temporary union...until Emily started showing him the joys of marriage—and love....

November 1999 THE PRINCESS AND THE COWBOY
Martha Shields (SR #1403)

When runaway Princess Josephene Francoeur needed a short-term husband, cowboy Buck Buchanan was the perfect choice. But to wed him, Josephene had to tell a *few* white lies, which worked...until "Josie Freeheart" realized she wanted to love her rugged cowboy groom forever!

Available at your favorite retail outlet.

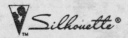

Silhouette®